CAVANAUGH JUSTICE: DETECTING A KILLER

Marie Ferrarella

HARLEQUIN

ROMANTIC SUSPENSE

HARLEQUIN®
ROMANTIC SUSPENSE™

Recycling programs
for this product may
not exist in your area.

ISBN-13: 978-1-335-73827-1

Cavanaugh Justice: Detecting a Killer

Copyright © 2023 by Marie Rydzynski-Ferrarella

For questions and comments about the quality of this book,
please contact us at CustomerService@Harlequin.com.

Harlequin Enterprises ULC
22 Adelaide St. West, 41st Floor
Toronto, Ontario M5H 4E3, Canada
www.Harlequin.com

Printed in U.S.A.

"Look, I *know* you have serial killers back in Southern California. They're not exclusive to New York City," Doyle said.

"I know that," Cassandra answered.

"Then I don't get it. Why are you so excited about this case?"

"First, it answers questions about what happened to our long-lost cousin, and second, there are endless possibilities regarding who the other victims were and why they were killed. Maybe we can find out what it was that they had in common that might have led to their demise."

"In other words, we resort to the usual."

"The 'usual'?" Cassandra questioned.

"Yes. Working hard, putting in long hours and juggling a ton of unanswered questions."

Cassandra shook her head. There was a depressing, hopeless note to Doyle's voice. "Oh, Detective, you have to be more positive than that."

"This *is* me being positive."

She stared at him in silence for a moment, and then surprised him as she began to laugh in response to his comment.

"If you say so," Cassandra said.

Dear Reader,

Here we are again at long last. Since we were last together, I came down with Long COVID—twice. For those of you who are lucky enough not to be acquainted with that version of the disease, at its height, it came very close to wiping out my mind. I have been writing stories since I was eleven years old, but for the first time in more years than I care to admit to, I found myself unable to write an actual sentence. Needless to say, I was panic-stricken. It was several weeks before I was able to concentrate enough in order to write absolutely anything, much less a book.

But I am back now, complete with a brand-new granddaughter (to go with my adorable two-year-old grandson), and I have returned to finally pick up the thread of another Cavanaugh story, complete with a serial killer. The story is set in New York City, my old stomping grounds. It is discovered that one of the Cavanaughs disappeared here when his divorced mother brought him to New York City from his initial home in Southern California.

Confused? I promise it'll all clear up by the time you finish reading the book.

As always, I thank you for reading one of my books (now more than ever) and from the bottom of my heart, I wish you someone to love who loves you back.

With affection,

Marie Ferrarella

USA TODAY bestselling and RITA® Award–winning author **Marie Ferrarella** has written more than three hundred books for Harlequin, some under the name Marie Nicole. Her romances are beloved by fans worldwide. Visit her website, marieferrarella.com.

Books by Marie Ferrarella

Harlequin Romantic Suspense

Cavanaugh Justice

Cavanaugh Vanguard
Cavanaugh Cowboy
Cavanaugh's Missing Person
Cavanaugh Stakeout
Cavanaugh in Plain Sight
Cavanaugh Justice: The Baby Trail
Cavanaugh Justice: Serial Affair
Cavanaugh Justice: Deadly Chase
Cavanaugh Justice: Up Close and Deadly
Cavanaugh Justice: Detecting a Killer

The Coltons of New York

Colton's Unusual Suspect

Visit the Author Profile page at
Harlequin.com for more titles.

To

Autumn Marceline Ferrarella

Welcome to the world, Little One

Love,

G-Mama

Prologue

Andrew Cavanaugh, the former police chief of Aurora, California, was finally about to sit down at the dining room table opposite his wife, Rose. He had just finished preparing a late supper for them, and for once, they were alone. It was a rare occurrence, given the numerous members in their family.

And just when he was about to pull out his chair, the doorbell rang.

Rose looked at her husband quizzically. He had already told her that they were going to be alone for a change. "Are you expecting anyone, Andy?"

It was meant as a tongue-in-cheek question, seeing as how there was hardly ever a time when they—especially Andrew—weren't expecting *someone* to drop by. The standing joke was that their home saw

so much foot traffic, it could have easily doubled as
Grand Central Station.

"I thought we were supposed to be alone tonight,"
Andrew replied. Resigned, the former chief of police
made his way toward the front door.

He moved like a much younger man, Rose caught
herself thinking with no small amount of pride and
not for the first time. Even after so many years together, she considered herself blessed. They'd been
in lockstep from the beginning, finishing each other's sentences and acting on the same thought. If he
went in another room, eventually she'd find him.
Always together and happy in the other's company.
Well, except for one long period when she'd lost her
way and forgotten how to get home. But Andrew
never let go, thank God.

Leaving her napkin on her plate, she followed
directly behind her husband, curious. One of their
younger relatives must be paying a surprise visit or,
more likely, was in search of a home-cooked meal.

When she reached him, Andrew had already
looked through the peephole and was in the process
of unlocking the front door.

His father, Seamus Cavanaugh, the former chief
of the Aurora Police Department and official family
patriarch, was standing on the other side of the door.
Seamus's usual deep, warm smile was conspicuously
missing. In its place was a look of deep concern.

"C'mon in, Pop," Andrew said, closing the front
door behind the gray-haired man. When he turned to

regard the older man, he felt he had a cause for concern. "I know that look, Pop. What's up?"

To his surprise—because his father loved to talk about everything and anything at the drop of a hat— Seamus Cavanaugh did not immediately answer the question.

"We were just about to sit down to dinner, Pop," Rose told her father-in-law, gesturing toward the table. "Join us," she said, inviting him in.

His father looked like a man who had just been caught in the middle of sleepwalking, Andrew couldn't help thinking. The man hadn't brushed his hair and looked as if he'd woken from a nightmare. Something was off and that worried him. Due to his advancing age, Seamus Cavanaugh had lost a little of his vim and vigor, but the light in his eyes had never lessened.

Until now.

This wasn't right.

At the very least, his father appeared troubled.

Andrew waited until his father had helped himself to several slices of pot roast and a healthy serving of mashed potatoes before attempting to engage him in conversation.

Seamus bathed the roast beef and mashed potatoes in gravy while totally ignoring the bowl of mixed vegetables awaiting his attention. Vegetables had never been the older man's favorite. The man groused often about how "leafy greens" were overhyped.

Andrew waited patiently until his father was finished putting his dinner together, then asked his question again.

"Okay, out with it. What has you looking as if you've just taken a large bite out of a particularly bitter lemon?" Andrew asked.

"Andrew, let your father eat," Rose chided, gesturing at her father-in-law's plate.

"I'm not telling him not to eat," Andrew said. "I'm just urging him to indulge in his second favorite hobby—talking. If he doesn't do that, he just might wind up hurting himself." When Rose raised her eyebrows, Andrew elaborated. "Keeping all that in."

He half expected his father to snarl at the remark. It was part of their usual give and take.

But this time, there was no snarling on the older man's part. There wasn't so much as a hint as to what had caused him to come over so suddenly.

The silence hanging between them seemed to go a great deal deeper than any situation warranted. Either his father wanted to concentrate on eating, or something was terribly wrong.

Andrew shifted in his chair, his carefully prepared dinner completely forgotten. "Okay, Pop, now you've really got me concerned. What's going on?" the former chief of police asked.

In response, Seamus sighed. Andrew was well acquainted with that sound. He braced himself for a long, involved story, one that would likely rob him of sleep.

Seamus rested his fork on his plate, then looked

from one member of the couple to the other. "Did I ever mention Nathan Cavanaugh to either of you?"

Rose shook her head.

"Not that I recall," Andrew told his father. It was not just a throwaway statement. The former chief of police prided himself on his memory. Had his father mentioned the name to him, even once, Andrew was certain that he would have remembered.

"I didn't think so," Seamus murmured, more to himself than to either person sitting at the table with him. "Nathan is the Cavanaugh nephew no one ever talked about. I hear that he was a rebel who always seemed to march to his own drummer." Seamus smiled sadly. "Making the family proud never seemed to be on his agenda. Instead of getting involved with law enforcement the way the rest of the family eventually did, or any sort of service-related way of life for that matter, Nathan just focused on having a good time."

Seamus looked as if every word he uttered pained him. "His father, Ethan, *was* in law enforcement, but he died in a traffic accident when Nathan was still a kid.

"As it turned out," Seamus said, continuing, "Nathan's mother, Barbara, never seemed to be all that up to the job of single-handedly raising a child. And she deeply resented Ethan's family—meaning us," he clarified, looking squarely into Andrew's eyes, "meddling in her life and her son's life. So, not long after Ethan was killed, Barbara took off with her son. Nathan was eleven at the time and was already getting into trouble."

"You couldn't find a way to stop her?" Rose asked, surprised. As far as she was concerned, the Cavanaughs had always been a force to be reckoned with. In addition to being a close-knit family, each member kept tabs on the other. If one was in dire straits, the Cavanaughs rallied around until the matter was resolved. Usually, it all ended in a massive family party. But maybe not this time.

"So, when Barbara and Nathan left, I thought it was better for everyone all around just to step out of the way," Seamus confessed. "I know that Brian," he said, mentioning one of Andrew's brothers and the current chief of detectives, "attempted to keep tabs on Barbara and the boy, but then they moved to New York City. Shortly after that, they proceeded to disappear off the face of the earth. That was approximately fifteen years ago."

"Not that I don't find all this fascinating," Andrew told his father, "but where is this going, Pop?"

The expression on Seamus's face turned grim right before Andrew's eyes. "Nathan's remains were just discovered, along with the remains of several other people, in a mass grave unearthed by a construction crew. The company was in the process of clearing a very large site of land. The idea was to build on it. That poor kid," Seamus lamented. "He never had a chance. We could have done something to stop this."

Andrew exchanged looks with his wife. Nothing was ever simple when it came to the family, he couldn't help thinking. His father's guilt alone warranted a few extra hours of consoling. But with this discovery about Nathan, Andrew understood that the Cavanaughs had to rally around one of their own, even if only to find out the real story behind his death.

"This just got a lot more interesting rather quickly," Andrew commented.

"Tell me about it," Seamus said, reaching for the bottle of wine next to him.

Chapter 1

"Are you sure the remains belong to a Cavanaugh?" Brian Cavanaugh asked his father the moment he walked in through the front door that evening.

Andrew had called him with the news. This was the first Brian had heard of Nathan Cavanaugh, resurfacing after all this time, but the chief of detectives supposed that anything was possible.

Andrew had called in both of his younger brothers to the house. Since their brother rarely invited anyone over without mentioning the words "impromptu party," Brian and Sean knew this had to be something serious.

They had lost no time in arrived at the former chief of police's house. Living close to one another, Brian and Sean arrived quickly, practically within two minutes of one another.

Seamus frowned at his sons. "Do the letters D-N-A mean anything to any of you boys?" he asked after giving each of his sons, including Andrew, a steely look that felt as if it had gone clear down to the bone. "With our collective experience in law enforcement, you'd think some of the brains would have rubbed off on you three."

Andrew sighed, digging deep for his patience. "Yes, Pop, we're all aware of DNA and the advancements made in the field of forensics since you were in your heyday."

Seamus shot his oldest a warning look. "Watch your tongue, boy."

"That goes both ways, Pop," Andrew said patiently.

"Okay, boys, back to your corners, or I'm sending all of you to bed without any dessert," Rose warned the men who were sitting around her table.

Seamus pretended to huff as he gave his oldest son a glare. "She's certainly become cheekier since she got back."

"She certainly has," Andrew confirmed with a laugh, giving Rose a one-arm hug.

Everyone at the table knew that the elder Cavanaugh was referring to the period of time that happened years ago. Andrew's wife had left the house to clear her head after they had had a rare argument, and due to a sudden, unexpected rainstorm, she had wound up driving her car into the river.

Swept away, she came very close to drowning.

The whole incident had given her amnesia. Because of that, she went missing for a number of years until fortuitous events had her crossing paths with her youngest child, Rayn, in the upstate diner where she had wound up working. Rayn immediately told her father, and Andrew quickly drove up to see for himself if this was the woman he had never given up hope of finding. It was.

Elated, he proceeded to work with Rose, and eventually, her memory did return.

"Never mind me," Rose instructed, knowing full well how very lucky she wound up being. "Just how sure are you that these bones that were uncovered actually belonged a Cavanaugh?"

"Very sure," Seamus assured his daughter-in-law. "The ME working the case is the grandson of an old friend of mine—and he has excellent credentials."

Andrew laughed softly under his breath. "'Of all the gin joints in all the towns in all the world, he walked into mine…'" the former chief of police murmured, allowing his voice to trail off.

"First of all, it's 'she,' not 'he.' And that's 'walks,' not walked," Brian told his older brother. "'She walks into mine,'" he quoted the movie line.

Andrew shot Brian an impatient look.

"Well, if you're going to quote it, quote it right," the chief of detectives told his older brother. "As for the sentiment, that still holds," Brian said. "Even across the country, there's no escaping the Cavanaugh penchant for getting involved in things."

It was Sean's turn to laugh. "That goes along with the fact that no matter which way you slice it, there are a lot of us."

"Apparently," Brian willingly agreed. "So, what's next? You want some of us to go and check out the validity of this story?" he asked. "That these bones actually belong to a distant member of the family?"

"My friend's granddaughter is no dummy," Seamus stated. He sensed that his sons were skeptical, but that didn't mean disrespecting the professionals. Just because it wasn't reviewed by a Cavanaugh didn't mean it wasn't legit. These remains were their blood.

"No one said she was incompetent, Dad. This is one of those 'trust but verify' cases," Sean told the others. "So, when do we go and collect these 'bones' and bring them back to bury in the family plot, where they belong?"

"I'm thinking that it's too soon for that," Andrew said to the others. "I'd hazard a guess that they're still trying to put the pieces together so they can figure out who killed these people and why."

"It's not just Nathan," Seamus told the gathering. "My guess is that they're trying to figure out who killed and dismembered the other people who were buried in that mass grave as well." His sons turned to look at him, which encouraged Seamus to continue. "I know I'm just an old man to you boys," he began, only to have Brian interrupt him.

"No one was saying that, Dad," Brian said.

"You didn't have to, boy," Seamus snapped. "It's

written all over your faces." When Andrew began to protest, Seamus held up his hand to silence his oldest, not wanting to get embroiled in a pointless argument. "But if you ask me, I would say that the collections of bones points to the fact that this could very well be the work of a serial killer. A very specific kind of serial killer."

It sounded like a viable theory, but Sean knew the danger of jumping to that conclusion too soon. They'd seen enough cases go south due to assumptions made on little to no evidence.

"What makes you say that?" Sean asked. His interest was thoroughly piqued, as always. He considered himself invested. Not only was Nathan Cavanaugh likely family, but a serial killer at large meant more victims.

"The number of dismembered bones that were discovered says it all," Seamus said.

"The entire area could have once been a cemetery," Andrew said, for once going with the simplest explanation, even though in his heart, he knew he was reaching.

"It could have been," Seamus magnanimously agreed. And then his green eyes narrowed. "But it wasn't."

"And how would you come to that conclusion?" Sean asked.

"That was the first theory that was considered and then discarded by my friend's granddaughter," Seamus answered.

"Your friend's granddaughter," Brian repeated. "Is she the one who came up with the serial killer theory?"

"It's not exactly a far-fetched theory," Sean interjected before their father could answer. His work in crime scene investigations had involved some rather heavy-duty crimes. It had shown him that there were more serial killers than he or anyone on his team was comfortable with. "Bear in mind that New York isn't some quiet, peaceful small town. At any given time, there are eight million people living in a rather small, crowded area. I assure you that they're not all going to be getting along," Sean said. "As a matter of fact, I'm rather surprised that New York City doesn't have *more* serial killers populating the area."

Seamus nodded his head. "That's putting it mildly."

There was something in his father's voice that caught Andrew's attention. "Do you know something, Pop?" he asked. "What's your angle on all of this?"

"Only that I've brought this rather troubling puzzle and placed it in the laps of possibly the best law enforcement officers the area has ever had the good fortune of possessing," Seamus told his three sons.

Andrew exchanged looks with his brothers. That had to be the most flattering thing any of them had ever heard coming out of their father's mouth—which instantly made Andrew suspicious. "The man is definitely after something," he declared knowingly.

All three turned toward their father and eyed him while they waited. Seamus appeared the soul of innocence, his eyes darting back and forth, as if about to deliver the mother of all assignments to them.

"Out with it, Pop. What are you looking for?" Andrew asked.

"That's simple enough. Closure." Seamus answered the questions so simply, he momentarily succeeded in shaming his sons for thinking there was something more sinister behind his motivation. "If this collection of bones does turn out to be a Cavanaugh, we owe it to the boy—and the family—to make the identification in person."

"And if he isn't a Cavanaugh?" Andrew asked, picking up on the way his father had phrased his statement.

Seamus considered the question for a moment, wanting to word his answer just right in order to motivate his sons. They had to join him on this quest. The idea that one of their own would lie in an unmarked grave turned his insides cold. Nathan Cavanaugh deserved to come home.

"We've all made our livings by pursuing justice, trying to bring it to the victims whose paths we've crossed as well as all the people we've come in contact with along the way. This isn't really any different than that. It just might wind up proving to be more personal," the senior Cavanaugh said.

"And if not, this is still part—I'm proud to say—of the service that we provide to the general public."

Seamus paused to catch his breath as he surveyed his sons, waiting for their confirmation. "Am I right?"

Andrew felt as if he spoke for all of them as he nodded his head. "You're right, Pop. So, what do you propose we do next?" he asked, aware that his father loved being consulted about procedure.

Seamus never hesitated. "I'd suggest sending a few of our people to offer their services to the NYPD to try to solve this case. I'm sure that, given the situation, they wouldn't turn down the help. We all have to help each other whenever we can. At any given time, they probably have more than enough to keep them busy without taking on a cold case—or several cold cases, as it looks like it's going to turn out," Seamus amended knowingly.

Andrew nodded, glancing toward his brothers. "Sounds like a good suggestion to me."

"You're already in the will, Andy. No need to kiss up to me," his father told him.

Andrew laughed, shaking his head. "There really is no getting along with you, is there, Pop?"

The remark was met with pseudo surprise on Seamus's part. "That *was* getting along with me," his father informed him. "And of course, now I'm hungry again. Go figure."

The four men chuckled, which was the moment when Rose chose to walk back into the dining room. She came in carrying a tray covered with five plates of coconut cream pie that she had prepared earlier. Years of being married to Andrew had taught her to always be prepared to feed any number of her husband's relatives at any given moment. She felt she couldn't go wrong with this dessert.

She looked from one man to another, her gaze stopping with her husband. "Is it safe to come in?" Rose asked.

"It was always safe to come in," Brian told his sister-in-law. "Especially for you."

"Let me rephrase that. Are you finished making negotiations?" she asked.

Seamus smiled. "They're all but set in stone, my dear," he assured his daughter-in-law.

"So, they agreed with you?" Rose asked, setting the tray down in the middle of the dining room table. It was a far smaller version of the one that Andrew often used when he held the family gatherings. Just a cozy, well-used cherrywood table for six. There had been decades spent sitting in this space and hammering out the problems of the world—and celebrating the joys of family.

"The boys' mama didn't raise any fools," Seamus assured his oldest son's wife with a broad, knowing smile.

"I'm sure you had a lot to do with their upbringing," Andrew's wife said with a wink. She had heard enough stories from her husband to know that her take on his and his brothers' upbringing was correct.

Seamus smiled broadly for the first time since he had crossed his oldest son's threshold this evening to deliver this unsettling piece of information.

"Andrew did very well hooking his star up to yours," Seamus told Rose, displaying very obvious approval.

"I'd say that we were both lucky," Andrew told his father, his eyes meeting his wife's.

Brian laughed, shaking his head. "Get a room, you two," he told the couple, pleased that the duo was still very much together.

It was Andrew's wife who answered him instead of Andrew. "We fully intend to just as soon as the three of you all leave," she informed her father-in-law and Andrew's brothers.

Seamus chuckled sadly. Lord, but he did miss his wife, he thought.

Months would go by without that old familiar feeling seeping into his bones and nibbling away at his gut. Even so, he never doubted that it was there, lurking in the shadows, waiting for him to let his guard down before it would finally pounce and take a chunk out of him.

It was the price a man paid for being fortunate enough to experience one great love in his life, Seamus thought philosophically.

Belatedly, Rose began to distribute the desserts, placing one plate before each of the men at the table and finishing putting one in front of her own space. She looked around at the men seated at the table.

"Can I get you boys something to drink? Coffee? Tea? Liquor?" Rose asked, going through what she had learned were the logical choices first.

"Sit," Andrew urged, rising to his feet as he said it. He nodded toward the men seated around them. "I'll water these heathens."

"You did the cooking—again," Rose emphasized. "The least I can do is distribute the dessert and get them something to drink so that you can go back to talking about this family member no one can remember ever meeting." She looked at Sean and Brian, "Although, one would think that you wouldn't have to go looking for something to occupy yourselves with, given that there is really enough for the police department to do right here in Aurora."

"This is family," Andrew told his wife in all seriousness. "And we never give up on family, no matter how much time might have gone by since he or she sat at this table," he said. For the time being, he was speaking hypothetically. "We will be there for them no matter what, when it really counts."

Rose nodded. There was no missing the message that her husband was leaving her.

She pressed her lips together. "I know," she answered.

And no matter what else happened, she would absolutely and endlessly always be grateful for that. Because if Andrew hadn't subscribed to that way of thinking, she might still be up north working in that sad little diner at the end of the road, feeling like there was a huge part of her life that was still missing—without having so much as a clue as to what it was and how to find it.

Rose found herself looking at Andrew and, for the umpteenth time that month, thought about how very lucky she was to have married Andrew Cavanaugh.

Chapter 2

It was a known fact that there were no real secrets within the Aurora Police Department. That fact was doubly true when it came to the Cavanaugh contingent that existed within the various sections of that police department.

The rumor went that something only needed to be *thought* about before it was conveyed from family member to family member at lightning speed.

That was, according to Brian Cavanaugh, only a standing joke of course, but there were times when the chief of detectives had his doubts as to just how much of a joke it actually was. So, when he called in a few members of his clan, his eyes swept over them, wondering if any of them knew why he had called them in, or if they were going to get ahead of themselves and *tell* him why they thought they were being summoned into his office.

Travis and Murdoch, the two young men, and Cassandra as well as Jacqui, the two young women, all part of the police force, looked amazingly similar to one another. There was no mistaking the fact that they were all related by blood.

The amazing thing was that they were all the product of two people who did not get along. In an era when few married people ever got a divorce, the couple did divorce when their sons were still young boys.

The boys' mother took the younger son, Murdoch, and went her own way while their father remained where he was, keeping the older son, Seamus. The boys grew up without ever interfacing with one another. It was a tragic reality of divorce, though both boys had grown into fine members of the Cavanaugh brood.

Two extra chairs were brought into the chief of detectives' office so that everyone was able to sit down for this meeting. Consequently, since there were four chairs in total facing the chief of detectives' desk, it was a little more crowded than usual. He went over to close the door and pull down the shades in case fellow detectives got too curious.

Brian then took his place behind his desk and smiled at the detectives facing him. The chief proceeded rather slowly, feeling the young people out.

"Do you have any idea why I've called the four of you in here?" he asked them, looking from one to the other.

He waited for someone to speak up, wondering if he would be interrupted immediately or if the young family members would be polite and wait for him to speak first.

Cassandra was the youngest of the late Angus Cavanaugh's offspring. She was also one of the quieter ones. But after working steadily six days a week without a break for close to nine months on what had initially seemed like a simple homicide case but wasn't, she and her partner had finally wrapped up the case.

Cassandra was more than ready for a break. She was planning on looking into taking a vacation the moment today was officially over. Heaven knew, she had the time coming to her. Her mind started to wander toward visions of a beach vacation and nothing but a thick book and a fruity cocktail with an umbrella. No, that wasn't really her style, was it? She'd be bored after twenty minutes.

And right now, she wanted to know why she was sitting here with her cousins. No one was talking, which put her nerves on edge. She had to say something. Now.

"Word has it you called us here because of what Grandfather Seamus discovered on his trip to New York City." Cassandra was only putting into words what the rest of her cousins had already been speculating about the moment they received the summons to come to the chief of detectives' office.

Secrets were extremely hard to come by, especially in her family, Cassandra couldn't help thinking.

"And what was it that he discovered?" Brian asked innocently, baiting the newly promoted detective who had more than performed admirably in the department. It was why she had initially secured that position in the first place.

Cassandra was aware that everyone in the room knew the answer to the question that the chief had just asked, but because Brian had never been anything but extremely fair without being unduly partial, Cassandra willingly played along and answered his question.

She dutifully recited what she herself had just recently discovered. "That Granddad Seamus discovered that there was a Cavanaugh that the rest of us were not really aware of and that his body had been discovered buried in what turned out to be a mass grave."

That was rather a vague explanation, but Brian was satisfied with it. "Word really does get around the ranks rather quickly, doesn't it?"

"We're detectives, sir," Travis Cavanaugh, one of the detectives attached to the fraud division, said, speaking up. "We detect."

"After all, it's in our blood," Jacqui, Cassandra's older sister, added to her cousin's assessment. "Not doing so would probably wind up driving us crazy, not to mention going against the laws of nature."

Brian nodded. He had expected nothing less from the young people sitting in his office. At this age, they were still all eager to solve crimes and every single mystery they came across. Time would teach them to savor those rare down moments when they did come around.

"I'm thinking of sending one or two of you to New York to find out what happened to this unknown, estranged Cavanaugh member—and why," Brian stressed.

"And what do you want us to do with the rest of the day?" Cassandra murmured under her breath, purely tongue-in-cheek. Accustomed to talking to herself, she didn't realize that her voice had carried.

But it did.

Brian's mouth curved. "Well, that will be entirely up to you, Detective," he answered, his eyes lighting up.

Startled, Cassandra looked up at the chief of detectives, the gist of his words sinking in. "Are you saying that you want me to go to New York to investigate?" she asked, stunned. She hadn't been expecting that. *Well, there goes that boring beach vacation— thank goodness.*

"Is there any reason that you wouldn't be able to go?" Brian asked. He glanced at the pages on the side of his desk, but there was no reason to review them. He already knew what was there, thanks to his ability for total recall. "I see that you have a lot of vacation time on the books, time you need to take before you lose it."

Cassandra shook her head. "No, no reason, Chief.

But going to New York would be kind of expensive. Prohibitively so," she added.

As a rule, Cassandra had always been careful with her money. It was one of the first things she could remember her father teaching her. He was very big on saving money, teaching his seven children to always weigh whether or not they could do without something rather than just spending money on it willy-nilly. And coupons. What wasn't to love about coupons? Cassandra kept a stack of them, feeling great satisfaction when she could present them at the grocery store.

Yeah, New York would likely drain her bank account.

"Cassandra, if you go, you would be going there as a police detective. The trip and everything associated with it would be covered and on the Aurora Police Department's dime—as long as you don't suddenly decide to go crazy spending," he added with a laugh. "And, from what I am told, going crazy isn't exactly your style.

"When all is said and done, you would be going to bring back Nathan Cavanaugh's body—or what there is left of it—so that it can to be buried in the family plot.

"Hopefully, along the way, you would be able to find out what happened to him. At the time Nathan went missing, I gather that his friends just assumed he disappeared of his own volition and not because something had happened to him."

Cassandra stared, amazed. "Does this mean I can order room service for every meal?"

Her cousins chuckled.

"Don't push it. But you should rest up and take care of yourself. This will be a tough assignment," Brian said. "And it's a sad story, no doubt about it."

Brian continued with a sigh, "Barbara, his mother had run off with the guy she had taken up with at the time." An unreadable expression passed over his face. "I hear she passed away not too long after that."

He didn't mention that it took a lot of detective work on his part to find that out, but the long-distance detective work he had put in did not yield what happened to Nathan at the time. Cassandra would likely dig up more information when she got to the city.

"Apparently," Brian said, continuing, "there turned out to be more to his disappearance than just that, since fifteen years later, Nathan has managed to turn up in small pieces in a mass grave along with the bones of what I was informed were several other people."

Brian's eyes met those of his daughter, Janelle. The only lawyer in the family, she had been called in for the meeting as well. He wanted to get her take on the matter.

"Did I get that right?" the chief asked his daughter innocently.

Janelle flashed a smile at her father.

"Yes," she confirmed. "As always, Chief." They

both knew that she was not there to rubber-stamp her father's actions but to make sure that he recounted them accurately and that the others in the room had no questions about what was happening. The last thing she wanted was to have her father sound as if he were making a mistake. Things like that, even in Aurora, had a way of blowing up.

Brian turned his attention back to Cassandra. "If I do wind up sending you to New York," he said, picking up where he left off, "do you think you can handle this assignment, Detective?"

So, he was being serious, Cassandra thought. She unconsciously straightened her shoulders as she answered, "Yes, sir. Absolutely."

I like her confidence, Brian thought as he nodded his head. "Good to know, Detective. Let me review a few more things, and I'll get back to you before the end of the day." He glanced around at the other faces surrounding his desk. "How about the rest of you? Any volunteers—or conversely, any objections to the idea of being sent to New York City? I grant you, it's not like Aurora. The weather's definitely a lot colder there these days."

"Might be nice to experience something resembling the seasons that the rest of the country faces," Murdoch commented.

"Said the man who never had to stand on the corner waiting for the bus in twenty-degree weather where the chill factor was down to five degrees," Brian said with a laugh as he looked at his nephew.

Janelle turned in her seat to look at her father. "And when did you have to face twenty-degree weather in New York?" she asked, curious.

"Not New York," he corrected. "But I was loaned out to the police department in Montana." He thought back, vividly recalling that time. "It was almost thirty years ago. At the time, they said it was the coldest winter on record." He laughed under his breath. "Anything you think is cold doesn't come anywhere near to the freezing weather in Montana. Not even close. I still shiver when I think about it," Brian admitted to the younger people in the room, all of whom had never experienced anything but the warm California sun.

"You're not exactly selling this assignment, Chief," Cassandra commented to the man. Maybe the beach vacation would be in order after New York City.

"Oh, where's your sense of adventure?" Brian asked good-naturedly.

She looked at her superior ruefully. "Solving that last crime wave was more than enough of an adventure for me, sir," Cassandra said to the Chief. Not to mention, New York was a city of eight million people, which meant it was crowded at all times. Cold and crowded didn't sound like a picnic.

Brian looked at the young woman, quietly studying her. Because of the number of his relatives that abounded in all capacities on the police force, he admittedly was more acquainted with Cassandra on paper than he actually was in real life.

In his opinion, she was being refreshingly honest right now. He had to admit that he would have thought that she would be chomping at the bit to be sent to the big city for free under the guise of taking care of business. That she appeared to be indifferent to the idea of experiencing all that without any actual cost to her surprised the chief, causing him to take an even closer look at her.

He had all but made up his mind to send her—but in his opinion, there was nothing to be gained sending her against her will if that turned out to actually be the case. There were enough capable people for him to choose from.

"Would you rather not go?" Brian asked Cassandra.

"It's not up to me," she told him in all innocence. "I will do whatever you and the job requires of me," Cassandra replied. *Even if it kills me.* She was a Cavanaugh, after all.

Brian sat back in his chair, quietly studying the young woman on his left. In his opinion, Cassandra had just managed to tilt the balance in her favor. That made her the right person for the job.

But this was not just some simple walk down the street or around the block.

This required a good deal more than that, and he did not want to have to be responsible for having to twist the young detective's arm in any way. He put his question to her as openly as possible.

"Do you have any objections to going to New York?" he asked.

Cassandra thought for a moment. "I've never been," she answered.

"I already know that," Brian told her. "But that doesn't answer my question. Would going to New York City present any problems for you?" he asked point-blank.

"I'll go if she doesn't want to or can't for some reason," Jacqui said, speaking up, all but waving her hand in the air in order to take her sister's place.

Brian's smile rose all the way to his eyes. "I think we all realize that, but your sister is the one with an abundance of vacation days that are all but crushing each other. It's the opinion of the personnel department that she needs to take the time before she winds up losing it. Vacation time does not accumulate indefinitely," the chief reminded all of the detectives seated before him.

His eyes turned toward Cassandra. "Now, unless you have some objection about going to New York on this assignment..." His voice trailed off as he waited for her to give him an answer one way or another.

She could just visualize her brother Morgan shaking his head and saying to her, "Where's your sense of adventure, Cass?" He'd be the first in line to try to prod her into going.

Though her job provided enough adventure for several lifetimes, Cassandra had never been any farther away from home than San Francisco. As many times as she thought about vacations, something always prevented her from seeing what else was out there. Maybe she was the one preventing herself from exploring outside of her comfort zone, which was the world of crime. Of course she needed to take part in this exciting adventure, especially if it would help the family.

She pressed her lips together. She didn't want the others, especially not the chief of D's, thinking that she was some sort of stick-in-the-mud who was willing to turn down a chance for a free trip to New York City. It was just that she was experiencing a little burnout.

But that would go away, she assured herself.

"Well, Detective?" Brian asked, waiting for his niece to give him an answer. He had the impression that he already had his answer, but he might just be jumping to conclusions.

Either that, or maybe Cassandra was afraid to grab at the chance he was offering her, and she really did want to go, but for some reason, she wasn't admitting that to him. Or for that matter, to herself.

Cassandra spoke slowly, quietly reviewing this opportunity she was being offered from all possible sides.

The more she thought about it, the more excuses began to melt away until they completely eluded her. It occurred to her that she had nothing concrete to offer the man she thought of more as the extremely capable chief of detectives than her uncle.

"No, sir," Cassandra informed him quietly. "I have nothing stopping me from going to New York City," she admitted. "As a matter of fact," she added, her voice growing stronger and more positive with each word she spoke, "I think that my going there to retrieve the long-lost member of our family is a wonderful idea."

"Terrific," Brian concluded with a wide smile as his eyes met hers. "So do I."

Chapter 3

Cassandra had just gotten off the elevator when she all but collided with Travis. Catching hold of her shoulders, her dark-haired cousin kept the slender young blonde from falling as he grinned at her.

"Just the person I was hoping to run into," Travis said. He had just left the chief of D's office and was holding a manila envelope in his hand. "I've picked up the plane tickets and all the other necessary information from the chief for that trip to New York City. I was just about to go looking for you."

"Well, you found me," she said, amazed that he was back at the precinct, much less that he had accomplished so much in what amounted to such a very short amount of time.

"I can see that," he answered, pushing onward.

"I thought that maybe we could catch a ride to LAX together."

She looked at him in surprise. Travis made it sound as if the details had been prearranged. "Did we talk about this?" she asked. If they had, it must have slipped her mind, she thought, annoyed with herself. But then, what with closing the old case she had been working and now thinking about the new one, she supposed that it was a little difficult keeping all her facts straight in her head at the moment.

"No," Travis said, "We didn't. But it only seemed like the logical way to go." He held up the envelope in his hand. "These are the plane tickets as well as the information about the hotel we'll be staying in and who to talk to at the Manhattan precinct about this case once we get there."

Cassandra suddenly felt as if she had somehow missed a step. She was used to being the one handling all the details, large and small. "Looks like you took care of everything that needed doing," she commented.

He had no intention of rubbing her nose in it. As far as he was concerned, this was her show. He was there just to help out—and to guard her, although he wasn't about to mention that part.

"I just got back before you did, that's all," Travis told her, then very quickly changed the subject. "Cullen's taking us to the airport. Unless you've already made other arrangements for us."

Cassandra shook her head. "No, not yet." She

looked at her cousin. "Apparently, you've taken care of everything." Cullen was one of Travis's older brothers and worked cases that came up in the Fraud Division. "I never realized that you were such an eager beaver."

Travis shrugged. "You've got to admit that this whole thing is out of the ordinary, and I guess that I'm just anxious to do the very best job I can. Who knows, this might even wind up leading to other things."

She took that to mean that he was looking into changing his career choice. She looked at him in surprise. "You're not happy in the division that you're in?"

"Oh, it's not that," he said, quick to deny her assumption. "I'm happy, but it never hurts to explore other possibilities." They were outside the building and heading toward the back parking lot. Changing subjects again, Travis told her, "I left my go-bag in my car."

"I did too—I left my go-bag in my car," she clarified, in case he thought that she had somehow gotten into his vehicle when she arrived. She glanced at her watch just as she saw Cullen's large beige car pulling up into the rear parking lot.

It was just a little after twelve o'clock. Traffic into Los Angeles was going to be absolutely awful, she thought, somewhat daunted. Most likely, it would be all stop and go.

"Are you sure that Cullen isn't going to mind driving us?" she asked. "Traffic is going to be in full swing."

"Cullen is usually up for absolutely anything," Travis assured her. "Why don't we collect your go-bag first, then we'll go get mine so we don't have to waste any of his time and get going?"

"Sounds good," Cassandra agreed. She was already heading to where she had parked her car. She expected to be making her way there alone, but she found that Travis was coming with her, shadowing her every step.

Cassandra couldn't help wondering if this was a sign of things to come, regarding their working together in New York. She honestly didn't know how she felt about that.

She had left her go-bag on the passenger seat next to the driver's side. She unlocked the door and opened it, which was when Travis leaned in and retrieved the bag for her. Looking at him in surprise, she found him grinning at her.

"I've got longer arms," he told her, handing it to Cassandra.

This was more than she was expecting. "I can carry my own go-bag," she informed her cousin rather crisply.

"No one's disputing that," he answered. "I just thought you looked a little tired and might want some help." He made no move to surrender the bag to her.

Shrugging, Cassandra decided there was nothing to be gained making a big deal out of what was, at bottom, courteous behavior. She knew for a fact that they had all been raised that way.

Locking up her vehicle, she pocketed her key. "Let's go get yours," she said.

At that moment, Cullen pulled his car up next to his brother and their cousin. He rolled down the window on his side.

"Your chariot awaits," he declared. Pulling up the handbrake, he got out of his car. "I can put that in the trunk for you, Cass," Cullen offered, taking Cassandra's go-bag from his brother.

"How do you know that's not mine?" Travis asked.

Cullen dropped the go-bag into his open trunk. "Because this go-bag doesn't look as if it's been through a war." He winked at Cassandra. "I know for a fact that Cass is a lot neater than you are, little brother," he said to Travis.

Turning on his heel, Travis retrieved his go-bag out of his trunk. The packed bag appeared dusty and badly in need of a cleaning. Packed tight, it was also straining at the seams.

"See what I mean?" Cullen asked Cassandra, pointing to his brother's bag.

Travis pretended to take offense at his brother's inference. "Very funny, wise guy."

"Just being observant," Cullen told Travis. Holding the passenger side door opened for Cassandra, he waited until she took her seat, then turned toward his brother who people had commented looked almost like his twin, except for being a little taller. "You get to ride in the back." When his brother frowned slightly, Cullen quipped, "Hey, it's either in the back or on the roof."

Sparing a glance at his passengers, Cullen paused before getting in on the driver's side. "You two all set?" he asked casually. "Nobody forget anything?"

"I think we're all ready to go," Cassandra told her cousin, then added with a warm smile, "You know you're going to make a great father someday, Cullen."

Travis rolled his eyes. "Don't encourage him, Cassandra. His ego's already the size of an ocean liner."

Cullen waved away his younger brother's comment. "Don't listen to him, Cass. You can say anything you want to me." He gave his brother what passed as a censoring look. "Travis already thinks he walks on water."

"Compared to you," Travis interjected pointedly, "I do."

Listening to the banter between her cousins, Cassandra realized how much she missed that sort of thing these days. Her five brothers were all married now, and between work and the separate lives they had established, she only got to see them occasionally.

Because she'd been so busy, she hadn't reached out to her brothers or their spouses enough. It was almost as if they lived on different continents instead of the same part of California. Part of her wished they would be in better touch with her, but they had their own lives. This happened when one partnered up; she understood that. How she wanted sometimes to belong to someone, to have one special person to talk to. But then, people like her were born to be 100 percent about their jobs. No time for other things. Right?

Cullen noticed the expression on Cassandra's face. "Everything okay?" he asked, sounding a lot more serious than he had when he had first arrived.

"Everything's fine," she assured Cullen. "Listening to the two of you just now, I remember how much I've missed my own brothers going at it like that."

Travis pretended to frown at her comment. "Don't encourage him, Cassandra, or he'll never shut up."

Cullen made a noise registering his displeasure over Travis's response. "Ah, you should talk," he told his brother.

"Well, yeah, I should," Travis agreed with no hesitation. "It's definitely preferable to listening to you doing all the talking."

Cullen glanced at Cassandra as he started up his vehicle again. "See what I have to put up with?" he complained, nodding at his younger brother.

She smiled at him. More accurately, at both of her cousins. "Yes, I do," she told Cullen. "And I have to admit that I'm a little jealous of that easy relationship the two of you have going for you."

"Speaking of being jealous," Cullen said, switching subjects easily. "I am."

"You want to back up a little there, big brother?" Travis requested. "What are *you* jealous about?"

Cullen glanced in his direction for half a second, "You're kidding, right?" he asked Travis, squeaking through the light as it went from green to yellow.

"Not that I know of," Travis answered, finding himself in the dark about his brother's comment.

Cassandra, however, knew exactly what her cousin was referring to. "I think he's talking about our trip to New York City," she said to Travis.

Travis leaned forward in his seat as he looked at his brother in surprise. "You never mentioned that you wanted to go to New York."

"What, you think I tell you everything?" he asked, feigning surprise.

Travis had another take on the subject. "You've never been quiet about anything," he said to his brother.

"You're getting me confused with yourself," Cullen told Travis matter-of-factly.

In response, Cassandra began to laugh. When Cullen came to a stop at the light, glancing in her direction for an explanation, she told both of her cousins, "You most definitely remind me of the way my brothers would go at it, dragging me into it when I least expected." Her expression grew wistful. "I had forgotten how much I really miss that time."

"Well, I just want you to know that you're welcome to hang around and listen to Cullen run his mouth off like that any time you like," Travis told her.

"Me?" Cullen questioned in surprise. "You should talk."

"I thought I was," Travis said to his older brother.

Cassandra crossed her arms before her as she sat back in the passenger seat and enjoyed what she thought of as "the show."

Without being conscious of it, the tension she had been experiencing for the last few weeks because of the case she had been working began to drain from her slowly and completely.

The traffic from Aurora to LAX was even heavier than it usually was.

Normally, she would have been worried that they'd arrive late to the airport and wind up missing their flight. But in this new, relaxed state, Cassandra just leaned back and let life unfold.

"I've forgotten just how overwhelming the traffic to LAX can be," Travis said, sitting on the edge of his seat and watching the way the cars and trucks crawled by, seemingly making their way by inches.

"Don't worry, I'll get you there," Cullen promised confidently. "We've still got time. The trick is to give yourself plenty of time to reach your destination without breaking a sweat."

"I wasn't aware that you could sweat, big brother," Travis said.

"I just made a point of the fact that I couldn't sweat. Weren't you listening, Travis?" he asked pointedly.

Cassandra could see the outline of LAX coming

into view, and she had to admit that she felt a sense of disappointment. Despite the fact that she knew they were supposed to reach the airport in time to be able to catch their flight to New York, getting to the airport meant that the show her cousins were putting on for her benefit—ragging on one another and bringing up memories of the way her brothers had been with each other around her—was sadly coming to an end.

Cassandra forced a smile to her lips, doing her best to seem carefree.

"Give me a call when you know when you're coming back to LAX," Cullen told her as he drove into the general lot. "I'll pick you up."

Travis spoke up, his voice breaking into his Cullen's thoughts. "I'm touched, big brother," he said.

"Yeah, I guess I'll pick you up too," Cullen said to him, sounding resigned. "But to be honest, I was thinking about just picking up Cassandra," he admitted.

Cassandra grinned. "You don't mean that."

"Oh yes, I do," Cullen assured her. He was approaching the terminal where their airline was housed. There wasn't a single parking space available anywhere near the terminal.

"Would you mind if I just let you off at the terminal?" he asked Cassandra. "It looks like it's going to be extremely crowded and impossible to park my car. I can either swing by and let you off at the entrance or park my car like several miles away so I can walk you two to the terminal."

"You'll do anything to get out of getting some exercise, won't you?" Travis cracked with a chuckle.

"Funny, I was thinking the same thing about you," Cullen told his younger brother.

Cassandra decided that she needed to call an end to this so-called dispute just in case it actually did get out of hand.

"Well, I for one think that dropping us off at the terminal is the right way to go. I have no desire to arrive in New York City exhausted and drained."

Cullen nodded. "Your wish is my command," he told his cousin.

The truth of it was that neither he nor his brother had any intensions of walking the long distance to reach their terminal. Pulling up at the terminal entrance, Cullen stopped his vehicle, allowing it to idle for several moments.

"Last stop," he announced. Remaining in the car, he popped his trunk so that they could retrieve their go-bags.

Travis lifted both his and Cassandra's go-bags out of his brother's trunk. Once he had them, holding them in one hand, he slammed the trunk shut.

Leaning his head out of the window, Cullen told both his younger brother and his cousin, "Have a safe flight."

It was Cassandra who flashed a smile at her

cousin as she said, "We'll definitely try our best, Cullen."

It was a promise that she intended to keep as she hurried toward the airport's electronic doors half a step behind Travis.

Chapter 4

"You're kidding."

Detective Danny Doyle of the Cold Case Division in a midtown Manhattan police department moaned in response to what Simon Lee, the man he had been partnered with on more than one occasion, had just said to him.

He looked at the detective whose desk was half a breath away from his, hoping to catch Lee grinning at him. That would mean that he was kidding.

But he wasn't.

On the contrary, Simon Lee had a very serious expression on his face. When a new case came in, Simon went from the jovial jokester to a serious and dangerous detective. Even though a few inches shorter and leaner than Danny, Simon could take down a fleet. And his partner knew how to lead him gently into bad news.

"Why would I kid about something like this?" Lee finally asked.

Doyle glared at the other man impatiently. "Because you have a sick sense of humor, and I'm up to my eyeballs in paperwork." If Lee was on the level, this was really going to impede his working on the case, not to mention everything else. "Whose idea was this, anyway?" Danny asked. He blew out a breath as his frown deepened. "This isn't funny, you know."

Danny took a deep gulp of his lukewarm coffee in the hopes that it would revive him.

"Nobody's laughing," Lee countered. "And from what I hear, the captain said to pass the word to the team that was identifying all those old bones that had been dug up at the construction site last week. That would be you—and me, as well as Davidson— but mainly you, because you caught this assignment first."

Danny blew out a breath. "Thanks for reminding me. It's yours if you want it," Danny told the other detective, raising his hands up as if to surrender all claim to the case. And then he looked at Lee more closely. "You're sure about your information? Because maybe you got it wrong," he suggested hopefully. "Maybe those California detectives were just calling here to get some information."

"No, they weren't calling for information," Lee

told the other detective. "From what I hear, there are two full-grown detectives descending on us. They're cousins, I'm told."

"Cousins?" Doyle repeated, shaking his head. "Great. So this is supposedly a family affair?"

"More than you think," Lee told him. "The detectives who are descending on us are not only related to each other; they're also related to one of the dead men whose bones were unearthed at that construction site."

Doyle rolled his eyes, and for a moment, he just closed them, gathering strength. "Oh, this is just getting better and better by the moment," he told his sometimes partner.

When a group of people descended on one small case, that didn't always bode well. There were turf wars, especially if you weren't familiar with the other detectives. But family intervening on a case? Not a good idea, even if the case was ice cold.

Danny didn't enjoy the idea of California detectives shadowing him, probably making annoying suggestions.

But then he thought for another moment. As a good detective, he had to examine the case from every angle. "Well, maybe we'll wind up getting lucky."

"How so?" Lee asked gamely, not sure where Doyle was going with this.

"Maybe they'll get lost between leaving JFK and getting here," Doyle suggested, then smiled as he thought the idea over. "At least, one can always hope."

Of course they wouldn't get lost. All it took was a tap on a phone before a car magically appeared to deliver parties to their destinations. No, these detectives would arrive safely and ready to go.

Technology had changed their profession by leaps and bounds over the last twenty years. Sometimes he complained about it, but most of the time, he was grateful, especially when solving cold cases. Still, he was irritated by the impending arrival of the California detectives.

"It's hard enough playing musical bones as it is without having to answer inane questions from people who are more interested in working on their tans than in finding out who's responsible for killing victims from over fifteen years ago—and why," Danny complained.

Not only did his quip amuse him, but he was also quite proud of the fact that he had done most of the legwork. He'd been able to date the bones that had been brought to his attention. It had definitely not been easy, but then he had never taken the easy way out.

Before he had ever gotten into the field of forensics, he would have never guessed that the human body had so many bones. The fact that he had wound up working with six bodies from over a decade and a half ago felt as if he were immersed in playing a mind-numbing game of fifty-two pickup, except that there were a lot more body parts involved than just that small number.

"Maybe you're being a little too hard on these California detectives," Lee said.

"They're coming in from California when they could have just as easily called in with their questions instead of disrupting my concentration." Danny shrugged. "Maybe I am being too easy on them."

He didn't take kindly to having his work interrupted.

"Sounds to me like you woke up on the wrong side of the bed. Did you?" Lee asked, curious, a wistful expression on his face.

Danny frowned. "If that's your subtle way of asking if I got any sleep last night, the answer is that I really didn't. This case has been eating away at me ever since those body parts turned up and landed in my lap," Doyle complained with feeling. "This case is definitely enough to cross my eyes."

At this point, Doyle was having trouble keeping his eyes open. The detective blinked twice, then dragged his hand through his hair. Things were beginning to look fuzzy to him. He was doing his best to focus. After all the time he had put in working this case, it was getting more and more difficult for him to be able to concentrate to do that.

Lee saw the tired look in the other detective's eyes and face. He wasn't used to seeing Doyle like this.

"Why don't you call it a day and go home, Doyle?" the other detective suggested. "You can come in and start fresh in the morning. Besides, something tells me that you're going to need all your strength and patience to deal with those body parts. I've got a hunch that we haven't seen the last of them. I think that stray bones are going to continue to keep turning up for a while longer," Lee said.

Danny was looking at this from an entirely different angle. "Those bones are probably going to be easier to deal with than those California dreamers who are on their way here," the detective reasoned. "Just why are they coming to New York, anyway?"

"From what I gather," Lee told his friend, "they're under the impression that one of the people we've dug up is a long lost relative of theirs. The guy went missing years ago, and his location was entirely unknown—that is until last week," Doyle said.

"You know," Danny continued, "I can understand wanting to identify a family member, but I can't see why we can't do it here for them. And once we pin down who might have killed the newly discovered family member, we can send them the body."

Lee looked at the younger detective knowingly. They had worked together enough times for Lee to be able to guess what was going through Doyle's mind.

"You just don't want them getting underfoot," Lee guessed.

"Yeah, there's that too," Doyle agreed matter-of-factly. "The way I see it, we've got enough people here in New York City. We don't need to bring in a couple more bodies to join in," he said, rationalizing.

"Maybe they'll turn out to be helpful," Lee suggested.

"Yeah, right." The look on Doyle's face said exactly what he thought of that speculation. Not much.

Lee laughed. "And maybe having the others spend a few hours in your company will cause you to drive these 'California dreamers' back to where they came from," the detective told his partner with a grin.

Danny shook his head, looking far from friendly. "One can only hope. Okay," he announced, turning off his computer. When the light went off on his monitor, he locked up his desk, "You've convinced me. I'm going to call it a day and go home."

"Calling it a night would be more accurate," Lee told the other detective. He had already turned off his own computer earlier and was now locking up his desk. "All right, I'll see you in the morning," he promised Danny. "Try not to come in with the roosters this time," he added.

Danny pretended to sigh, feigning disappointment. "Well, I guess there go my plans for the morning," the younger detective said.

"Very funny," Lee said, then pointedly told Doyle, "See you in the morning."

The fact that there might be more unaccounted for body parts out there kept Danny Doyle up for most of the night.

You would think, the detective reasoned to himself, *that after going through the dismembered limbs for more than a week, I would have gotten used to sifting through them by now.*

But that just wasn't the case. At least not yet. All those unaccounted for limbs still comprised a mystery to him.

Well, at least one dismembered individual would be going home soon, Danny told himself. He supposed he could call that a win. A couple of other body parts had finally been identified as well, but not all of them. The only thing that had been identified was the manner of death. Obviously, to him that manner was homicide. The way the individuals had been killed and dismembered led Danny to believe that this was the work of the same serial killer, one that might still be active.

At least that knowledge was something, Danny thought, comforting himself. Now all he needed to do was find out who was responsible for these deaths, which was not nearly as easy as it sounded. Killers could come and go on a whim, though with updated technology, they had more ways to find them. There were fewer places to hide, especially in a city with top notch security.

Yeah, he could solve this case, provided that he didn't make a mistake.

Danny stopped at the café in the lobby and picked up his morning coffee. Something told him that he would need to treat himself to an extra large cup of the strong brew before facing these so-called detectives from California.

He just hoped he could hold on to his temper. He

didn't like being told what to do. Over the years, he'd learned to swallow the resentment if someone went too far trying to step on his work. He wanted to move ahead and get the job done. This case might take extra restraint on his part.

Rather than the elevator, he decided to take the stairs to the fourth floor. He was a firm believer in getting his exercise in whenever possible.

Danny glanced at his watch when he reached the third floor. Despite all his efforts to catch a few extra minutes of sleep, he had still managed to get into the office early. There was something about the bodies that had been retrieved that still bothered him. He felt as if he had somehow failed to address something right out there in plain sight, but for some reason, he kept missing it.

But what?

It did not exactly put him in a good mood.

He supposed it was probably all just his imagination. There were times when he almost felt that there were serial killers hiding within every nook and cranny. Other times, he felt as if he were just letting his imagination get carried away. The one thing he wouldn't have ever believed until he became part of the police force was that there were so many of these killers out there, people who thought nothing of snuffing out a life.

That was because New York was a big city, he told himself as he walked into the Cold Case Squad

Room. At this time of the morning, Danny expected to find the area fairly empty. And it was.

Except for the gorgeous blonde sitting one desk over from his. She wore a sleek gray suit, and her thick hair fell about her shoulders. Obviously, she was a supermodel or a test to see if he could be distracted. Just his dumb luck.

Assuming this was the woman who had come in from Southern California, he looked around for her companion. But the very stunning woman appeared to be quite alone…and waiting just for him. This had to be a dream come true or the universe's idea of a cruel joke.

Walking in toward his desk, he set down his sealed coffee container in the middle of the desk, took off his jacket, then draped the jacket over the back of his chair.

"Can I help you with anything or find someone for you?" he finally asked the woman after briefly making eye contact with her. Her large green eyes slayed him.

"That all depends," she replied.

"On?"

"On whether or not you can point me toward Detective Danny Doyle."

For a second, he thought she was kidding, then he realized that she was being serious. Not once did she look away from him, which was unnerving, to say the least. Obviously, this was how she got criminals to confess their bad deeds.

He glanced around to see if Simon Lee was somewhere hovering in the shadows, maybe to save him from his inevitable downfall. When he didn't appear to be, Danny still made no reply, but what he did do was raise his hand and silently point it to himself.

"You're Detective Danny Doyle?" she asked him, surprised.

"I am."

"Wow, what are the odds?" she marveled. He found the smile that rose to her lips absolutely mesmerizing.

Did she have any idea how lethal she was to him right now? He felt an urge to sit down but resisted it. Talk. That's what he had to do. Put words together and say them.

"I always thought they were pretty good, seeing as how that was the name on my birth certificate. I take it that you're the detective from Southern California who's come here to claim the body of your relative."

Cassandra nodded, putting out her hand toward him. "I am. Detective Cassandra Cavanaugh, at your service," she said.

He shook her hand, hoping his grip wasn't too clammy, given how she started to make him sweat.

"Wasn't there supposed to be one more of you?" he asked, looking around.

He wasn't prepared to hear her laugh in response. "Did I say something funny?" he asked.

"There are actually a great many of us," she told

him. "There are times that I feel like we comprise half of the Aurora Police Department."

Her lighthearted tone charmed him. Danny felt less on edge and more curious, which could be her way of trapping him into liking her. It was working. "Your whole family isn't here, right?"

"No." Cassandra got a kick out of the expression on his face. "They're back in Aurora, minding the store."

"So, you came alone?" he asked. Maybe saying that there were two of them coming had been a mistake.

"No, not alone. The chief of police insisted that my cousin come along with me, so there're two of us here."

Danny scanned the squad room for a second time, thinking he might have missed seeing the other detective.

But he still came up empty. "So, where is he?" Doyle asked, suddenly fidgeting with his hands.

"He's presently down in your cafeteria. Detective Cavanaugh wanted to stop for breakfast. He should be up here in a few minutes," she promised, saying, "Travis eats fast."

"Travis?" he repeated, wondering if he had heard her correctly. The heat had just turned on in the precinct, and the cycling noise temporarily blocked her out. He instantly felt the room getting warmer.

"My cousin," Cassandra clarified, raising her voice. "When we came to the precinct and explained what we were doing here, one of your officers escorted us into the building. An Officer Saunders," she recalled. "He asked us if we wanted to get something to eat or drink, and my cousin Travis is a walking bottomless pit, so naturally, he said yes."

Cassandra gestured around the area she was sitting in. "I wanted to come up here and get acquainted with whoever is dealing with the bodies that had been dug up." Her mouth quickened. "In other words, you," she told Doyle. "My cousin will be here soon," she said. "Travis hardly chews his food. He just swallows."

"Doesn't exactly sound like a pleasant experience," the detective commented.

Cassandra shrugged. "I wouldn't think so either," she agreed, "but from what I've been able to ascertain, eating that way seems to make Travis happy."

Danny frowned, more to himself than at the woman he felt he was being saddled with. He raised and lowered his shoulders in an utterly careless gesture.

"Whatever makes the man happy," the detective commented.

"Trust me, you wouldn't want to have to deal with Travis when he's hungry. It's not exactly the most pleasant experience," she said, then grinned. "Picture trying to carry on a discussion with a hungry bear. A very grouchy hungry bear."

Danny gave her a look, wondering if she was kidding or just telling tales out of school for some unknown reason. Whatever happened to presenting a united front? Or hadn't these Californians heard of that?

Probably not, he caught himself thinking. He doubted that they were even capable of thinking. The part that irked him most was how she felt so comfortable sitting next to his desk first thing in the morning, as if she'd been here before and owned his turf.

Even though this person was alluring as hell, he couldn't deny his resentment. This was *his* case, and no amount of easy charm could sway him from that fact.

Chapter 5

Cassandra could see by the detective's expression that he was more than a little skeptical. "You don't believe me, do you?" she asked him good-naturedly.

It was difficult for her to breathe, but she forced herself. The man she'd be working with couldn't have been more handsome if she'd dreamt him herself. With his short brown hair, blue eyes and rugged stance, he looked like he'd walked out of an action-adventure movie. And yet, something about him seemed tired. New York tired. She didn't know him, but obviously, he'd been working hard and not getting enough sleep. In such a busy city, she could see getting lost in the whir of activity, especially when dealing with murder. And the detective certainly didn't want to mince words with her.

His expression grew dour. "It's not a matter of not believing you."

"Then what is it?" Cassandra asked, curious. Her blunt question managed to throw Doyle completely off guard.

The suspicious look in his eyes intensified. "Just why are you telling me any of these mundane things?" he said. "We need to focus on the case, like now."

"I'm just painting a broader picture for you," she told him, then added, "or filling in the blanks so you can get to know a little more about the dead man. Take your pick," Cassandra said, flashing a thousand-watt smile at him. She was determined to break through the glass wall he seemed to have erected around himself in order to keep her out.

Two things she'd learned from her work: (1) Cheerfulness went a long way. She'd managed to warm up the iciest of colleagues with a kind word. (2) Always be the last one standing. She could wait out even the most stubborn person, and she sensed that this guy wanted to play only by his rules. That did not make for a good team.

Could this detective be too stubborn even for her? The next few seconds would tell.

And then Danny blew out a breath, showing her once again the virtue of patience. "What I'd like to find out is what there was about your relative that would single him out to a serial killer, making his death more appealing over someone else's for some reason."

"And you're sure that this is the work of a serial killer?" Cassandra asked him.

It sounded like a challenge to him—and not one without merit, he'd give her that—even though he didn't really want to. "Right now, I'm not sure of anything, but it's beginning to look that way," Danny said.

And then he sighed. It occurred to him that he wasn't being fair about this. That was what happened when he didn't get his required twelve and a half minutes sleep a night, he thought impatiently. People in his line of work took sleep for granted, never realizing how crucial it was for brain function.

"Sorry, I didn't mean to jump all over you like that," Doyle said.

Since he apologized, she waved the offense away. "Don't worry about it. I have five brothers," she told him. "It would take more than a misplaced curt word or two to hurt my feelings." Cassandra smiled. "We Cavanaughs are a lot tougher than we look."

"I'll remember that. Provided we work together long enough for that to matter," he added as a postscript.

She interpreted his words in her own way. "So, I take it that you're on the verge of wrapping this up quickly?"

Danny laughed under his breath. She was a sharp one. In his own fashion, he could admire that. "One can always hope."

"Funny," Cassandra couldn't help commenting,

"you didn't strike me as someone who would be acquainted with something as nebulous as hope."

"Why?" he asked, pinning the California invader with a penetrating stare. "You don't know a thing about me."

A lopsided smile had slipped over her face, curving her lips. One skeptical eyebrow rose. "Are you sure about that?"

Just one question, and she leveled him. This case would be a challenge, for sure. But this intriguing new element might devastate him. Just yesterday, he hadn't known that Cassandra Cavanaugh even existed. He hadn't known that this woman and her cousin were descending on the precinct until just late yesterday. Danny assumed that when it came to that, it was a two-way street, which meant that she hadn't known anything about the people she was descending on either.

"Yes, I'm sure," Doyle told her after a beat.

Just before she and Travis had left, the chief had told her what and who to expect as part of her welcoming committee. In addition, she was also blessed with the kind of memory that never allowed anything to slip away into the recesses of her mind once she became aware of it. Especially when it had something to do with her family—and the idea of a serial killer being involved in this somehow only made it doubly so.

The moment she had learned the name of the detective in charge of this case, she immediately educated herself regarding Detective Danny Doyle. The internet was a wonderful place for that. She had found all sorts of interesting things about him.

Cassandra's smile widened even more. She took a breath and launched into her recitation. "Okay, here goes. You put yourself through school by holding down two jobs. You took on a third part-time job to help support your mother when she had to stop working because she had leukemia. Any extra money you made went to pay her bills—until the day she passed away.

"Your biggest regret," Cassandra continued as he looked at her, stunned, "was that she didn't live long enough to see you graduate from the police academy—but she knew," she told him with certainty. "Trust me, she knew."

That was much closer to home than he was comfortable with. Doyle frowned. "You pretending to be some kind of clairvoyant?" the detective demanded.

"No, just a believer," she informed him with a soft smile. "You also have a tendency to keep your distance from people. That's an obvious effort to keep from getting hurt."

He was surprised at how dead-on accurate this detective from California was. Someone must have fed her the information. But who? And why?

"Not bad," Doyle told her coldly, inclining his head. "And just what am I thinking right now?" he challenged, his eyes meeting hers.

Cassandra laughed, her expression turned just a

touch somber as she shook her head. "Oh no, I don't use that kind of language," she told him seriously.

Doyle's eyes widened for a moment, and then he began to laugh, as if the revelation she had just made was dead-on and wound up utterly tickling him.

It was Cassandra's turn to be surprised. "You *can* laugh," she noted. "I didn't think that was something you were up to."

The laugh had just slipped out. Doyle backtracked. "Don't get used to it." he warned.

"I'll try hard not to," Cassandra answered, doing her best to sound solemn. Then she blew that all to hell when she added, "But you should know that you really do have a great smile. And that it interferes with your big bad wolf image."

"I'm not moved by empty words."

"That's good," Cassandra responded, "because I don't believe in using them."

A movement at the far end of the room caught her eye and she turned toward it. She discovered that Travis had picked that moment to walk into the squad room.

"Thank you," he said to the officer who had escorted him to the area. The moment he saw Cassandra, Travis's face lit up. "You *are* here," he declared as if finding her represented his journey's end.

"Certainly looks like it, doesn't it?" Her eyes dipped lower to his waist. "You get enough to eat?" Cassandra asked her cousin.

Travis smiled broadly and nodded. "They've got a

great cafeteria, Cass. Doesn't hold a candle to Uncle Andrew's kitchen, of course, but then, nothing really does," he acknowledged. "Still, I can't complain."

"Detective Doyle," Cassandra said, assuming a formal tone as she turned toward the man she had been talking to, "I'd like you to meet my cousin, Travis Cavanaugh. Travis, this is Detective Danny Doyle. Looks like we're going to be working with him."

Danny felt as if he were listening to his own death sentence being recited. Now there were two Cavanaughs in his squad room. That couldn't be good.

Travis put his hand out toward the detective. "You don't look overly happy about working with my cousin," he noted with an understanding grin. "Don't worry, she'll grow on you."

"Like fungus?" Danny couldn't help asking. The words seemed to find their way to his lips automatically.

Rather than take offense for his cousin, Travis exchanged looks with Cassandra as he laughed. "How long were you up here with him?"

"Not that long," Cassandra answered innocently.

"Man must be a quick study," Travis said.

And then Cassandra got down to business. "He thinks that Nathan might have run afoul of a serial killer," she told her cousin.

"What I said," Danny interjected pointedly, "was that it was one possibility."

"Well, for lack of anything more concrete to send

us in another direction, I'd say that this is as good a direction as any to start out with until something better turns up," Cassandra said.

"Around here, we don't just jump at the very first thing that comes along," Danny told the visitors.

Cassandra flashed a patient smile at the detective. "Good thing that we came along when we did; otherwise, these body parts might have gone back into the ground again, rotting for another twenty years, if not more."

Irritation creased Doyle's brow. "We don't rebury evidence."

"Good, then let's go on trying to identify who these body parts belong to and just what their last movements were before they became *disjoined* body parts," Cassandra said.

Exasperation creased Danny's brow. Why did every word out of this woman's mouth irritate him this way—because there was no denying the fact that it did.

"Is she always this annoying?" Danny asked her cousin.

Travis congratulated himself for not laughing out loud. "Hell, no. This is one of her better days," he told the other man. "You should see what she's like when she's going full steam ahead."

Cassandra shot her cousin an irritated look. "I can speak for myself, Travis."

Travis gestured with a flourish, encouraging her to continue. "Then go right ahead, Cass."

Cassandra turned to the detective who was supposedly hosting them, knowing full well that if it was up to him, they'd be boarding a plane, bound for Aurora, California, right at this instant. The more he warned them off, the more she wanted to dig in her heels. Not only for professional reasons, but also it struck a personal chord for her entire family.

"Have you managed to identify who the other bones belonged to, other than our long-lost cousin?" she asked.

"Our forensic pathologist is running tests, doing her best to put a name to the pile of bones we retrieved. At the moment, she's managed to place them into six separate piles, and so far, we might have names for four of the piles. One for certain—your long-lost cousin," he said. "The other three piles have temporarily been identified. That leaves us with two unidentified piles of bones still in need of names. But it's just going to be a matter of time."

"That sounds promising. Why don't we divide up what we have at the moment?" she suggested. She realized that she was usurping Detective Doyle's position, but when she got excited, she just couldn't help herself. "If these people have any relatives around, we can start asking questions, eliminating possibilities." She could see the reluctance in the detective's eyes. "It beats sitting around, watching our nails grow."

"I thought we were the ones with the reputation of jumping in with both feet?" Danny said, referring to the fact that supposedly, outsiders felt that New Yorkers got ahead of themselves.

Cassandra laughed. "We just let you think that. That's mostly for camouflage," she confided. "Mostly, we observe and make mental notes—and then we lay traps. Real ones."

Danny sighed, taking a folder out of his drawer. "It's times like this that I regret not following my first dream," he murmured, mostly to himself.

He should have known better. By the look on Cassandra's face, he had managed to pique her curiosity. "Which was?" she asked the detective when he didn't elaborate.

It was obviously too late to take back what he had just said. "Becoming a fireman."

"A fireman?" Cassandra echoed seeming mildly intrigued.

"Yes," Danny bit off.

"How old were you?" she asked, trying to put this in the proper perspective.

"Doesn't matter," Danny told her, dismissing her question.

"It does if you were five years old at the time," Cassandra countered.

Doyle looked at her, surprise registering on his face.

"Not bad," he said. He knew that piece of information hadn't made it into any file. That had to be pure intuition on her part. "Is that your gut talking?"

She placed a spread-out hand over her stomach

as if to press back any possible rumbling sound that might have risen to the surface. "I certainly hope not," Cassandra quipped.

"Do you charge extra for the comedy act?" Danny asked cryptically.

"Nope," she informed him with a grin and then winked at him. "That's on the house."

It was an odd time for him to notice that her eyes, which were an incredible shade of green, were sparkling as she looked at him, but nonetheless, he did. It caused the cryptic words that had risen to his lips in response to temporarily fade away.

"If you don't mind," he heard himself saying, "I'd rather that drinks were on the house, not your comments."

"Tell you what, we identify all six sets of bones and bring this case to a satisfactory end, and I'll definitely spot you those drinks," she promised.

Danny's eyes met hers. "All right," the detective told her, then he shifted to look at the man who had come with this annoying woman.

As if on cue, Travis turned to him. "Don't worry, Cassandra has always been as good as her word."

Danny wasn't at all convinced. Still, he couldn't exactly come out and contradict the detectives that had descended on his precinct—and him as well. It didn't make for a good working relationship—however long that was going to last.

And he hoped not long. With luck, by the end of the week, this irritating woman and her partner would stop disrupting his life and be on their way back to where they came from.

He just had to last that long, he thought. That meant hanging on to his temper. That was not as easy as it might seem, Doyle couldn't help thinking.

Gritting his teeth, he managed to squeeze out the words, "I certainly hope so."

Travis felt that the response merited one from him.

"There's no reason to doubt that," he told the New York detective, coming to his cousin's defense. "Trust me, there's no reason at all."

Chapter 6

The newscaster's voice echoed ominously in the dark, all but empty apartment, eerily recounting a story about the number of skeletal bones that had just recently been unearthed, thanks to a construction crew clearing through an old, long-neglected site.

"The site has incurred a temporary work stoppage until the bones that were found—overwhelming in number—can be identified." Pausing, the young woman took in a deep breath. "Progress unfortunately is very slow due to the weather conditions," the pert newscaster added.

The man who was bent over the coffee table, intent on consuming the omelet he had made, stopped eating. He raised his fork from the plate and used it to give the reporter a mock salute.

"Yeah, well, good luck with that," he said, laughing under his breath.

He was more than well acquainted with all the bones that had been found at the site. Was responsible for not only all of them but the manner in which they had been laid out. He had documented them all in his head—doing it on paper was far too dangerous and incriminating. But no matter, he was the only person who mattered here.

After all, he had been the one to have laid these men to rest in the first place.

These men as well as so many others.

He hadn't expected for the bodies to have been discovered for a very long time. That they had been after all his precautions was a real surprise. But that was neither here nor there. After all, he hadn't done it for the notoriety in the first place. At least, not at the time. He had done it because each and every one of those pretty boys that he had skinned and buried had had it coming to them.

As he thought about it—lost in a world of his own making—he paused as he savored the last of the omelet he had made—just the way he had been taught to do all those years ago.

The taste of the omelet reminded him of the child he had been—and the way his mother had always made him clean his plate.

Insisted on it, really. Otherwise, he was not allowed to get up from the table. Instead, he would be forced to sit there no matter how long it took to finish his meal. Sometimes that meant hours on end. A few times, he'd spend the night sitting at the table and staring at his uneaten food. Then, his mother would find him in the morning and yell at him to clean up and go to school. Those memories haunted him. Maybe not haunted, he amended, but inspired him to lead life the correct way.

He could still hear his mother's voice in his head. *Don't you want to make your mama happy?* she had demanded. *Well, don't you?* she had asked, her voice growing more and more shrill when fear of his mother had stolen the words from his lips.

He had been small for his age and was very easily intimidated.

Until the day that he wasn't, he recalled with a tight, satisfied smile.

He spent a few moments reliving the memory of that day in the dark recesses of his mind before he rose to clear away his empty plate.

He would have rather just left the plate where it was for now, but again, he could hear his mother's voice in his head, reminding him, *Messes don't take care of themselves, you know—and I'm not your maid, Pretty Boy. If you think that, well, you just have another think coming.*

A shiver went down his spine as he did his best to banish all thoughts of his mother from his mind. Instead, he kept his eyes on the screen, absorbing every single nuance of the news as he washed his plate, utensils and frying pan in the sink.

If anyone could see him now, they wouldn't notice a thing out of place—just a guy rotting in a small room with its peeling wallpaper and fetid air. The whole city was a decomposing body; so much so, it was easy to go forgotten. Just one wrong turn and his past showed up on the news. But then, no one would be able to find him, and he didn't need a lot of space to continue his work.

A sense of satisfaction slowly marched through him.

"How's the medical examiner coming along with making the IDs on the bones that had been unearthed?" Cassandra asked as she walked beside Travis, following Detective Doyle to where the young ME was faced with trying to make sense of what amounted to a bone jigsaw puzzle.

Walking into the room, she had taken note of the fact that there were collections of bones laid out on the various tables. At first, there seemed to be no rhyme or reason to it. But then, as she studied the various tables, she saw that four of them held what appeared to be approximately the same number of bones, more or less neatly arranged in some semblance of order, while the other two tables were not nearly as filled yet.

The jigsaw puzzles on those tables appeared to be in the middle of being sorted. None of those puzzles seemed close to complete, certainly not nearly ready to be identified, the way the bodies arranged on the first four tables were.

"Works in progress," Cassandra murmured to herself, doing her best to focus on the final outcome. Just discovering the fact that the compilation of bones appeared to be the work of a serial killer was a big deal. Whatever came after that could be viewed as a bonus.

Like nailing the killer who was responsible for these deaths.

"Baby steps," Cassandra said in an effort to comfort herself. She hadn't meant for the words to slip out, but they obviously had.

Danny looked at her over his shoulder. "Did you say something?"

Oh, no, she wasn't about to admit to that. Cassandra could just anticipate this sexy detective's critical comments. She was not about to give him the chance to laugh at her.

"Nothing that bears repeating," she told Danny lightly, silently adding, *At least, not for the time being.* She intended to forgo that conversation until much later.

But apparently, the New York detective was not ready to drop the conversation just yet.

"Oh, I'm pretty sure that you did say something," Danny told her, humor curving a mouth that, at rest, could be described as being more than generous. The look in his eyes silently told her that he was waiting for her to own up to what he was saying.

"Sorry," she told him. "I'm afraid that it just slipped my mind." She switched her focus slightly. "I'm really anxious to find out what we have on these people and how we can tie them to this being the work of a serial killer." She took a deep breath. "Where can we begin?"

The detective glanced at Cassandra's cousin and then at her. He had to admit that he had not been in the presence of this sort of blatant enthusiasm since—well, he really couldn't accurately pinpoint exactly when he had been confronted with this sort of eagerness to arrive at such needed answers.

Possibly never.

In New York, it was easy to burn out after a few brutal cases. After years, he'd seen the light go out of several colleagues' eyes. He just hoped he could muster the same workaholic tendencies and keep going until he felt his work was done. Maybe being around these two detectives was a good thing, though he couldn't admit this out loud.

"Look, I *know* you have to have serial killers back in Southern California," he told the cousins. "They're not just exclusive to New York City."

"I know that. They most definitely exist in California," Cassandra answered before Travis could say a word.

Danny blew out a breath as he shook his head. "Then I don't get it. Why are you so excited about this case?"

Cassandra never hesitated. "Number one, it answers questions about what happened to our long-lost cousin, and number two, there are endless possibilities regarding the other murders as to who the victims are and why they were killed." She looked at the detective. "If we find out who these victims are, maybe we can find out what it was that they had in common that might have led to their demise."

"In other words, we resort to the usual," Danny told the visiting detectives.

"The usual?" Cassandra questioned.

"Yes. Working hard, putting in long hours and juggling a ton of unanswered questions," Danny said.

Cassandra shook her head. There was almost a depressing, hopeless note to Doyle's voice. "Oh, Detective, you have to be more positive than that."

"This *is* me being positive," he answered.

She stared at him in silence for a moment and then surprised him as she began to laugh in response to his comment. Obviously, Danny Doyle wasn't used to uplifting banter in any way. He was a pessimistic, just-the-facts kind of man. She usually didn't find this at all charming, but this one man tickled her. Yes, he made her laugh, maybe without trying.

"I believe you," Cassandra said. Taking a deep breath to attempt to regain her composure, she got down to business. "Do you have any reports or paperwork attached to any of these people?" she asked, waving her hand at the tables with their various collections of arranged bones.

Danny laughed to himself in response to her question.

"Something funny, Detective Doyle?" Travis asked. He was attempting to field the question for his cousin. He wasn't sure if this New York detective was just being callous or if there was something more at play here, but whatever it was, if it did turn out to be callous, he had been sent by the chief of detectives to protect her, and protect her he fully intended to do.

"I think that your cousin is the only detective I've ever heard referring to a collection of bleached bones as 'people,'" Danny admitted.

Cassandra examined the bones that had been laid out on the closest table and then looked at him in mild surprise.

"Well, they were people—once. The body parts on these tables represent someone's husband, lover, significant other, son, father... You name it, the possibilities are endless," Cassandra said, the look on her face challenging him to say otherwise.

Danny inclined his head, looking at the various bones spread out on six tables. "You are assuming that they were all males," he said. Other than the identification of her cousin, no one had said anything one way or another about these victims being men. "Why?"

Cassandra shrugged. "Call it a gut feeling," she replied guilelessly.

Travis glanced at the other detective, a touch of pity entering his eyes. He had just watched the New York detective slip unknowingly over toward his cousin's side, even if he didn't realize it. The man was a goner.

Cassandra's cousin glanced toward the medical examiner. The woman appeared to be totally enjoying the show from the sidelines.

Danny looked at the ME. The woman had been silent and appeared to be all but bursting to say something. "Do you have anything to add, Dr. Wade?" he asked, encouraging the woman to add in her two cents.

"Well, personally, I think this killer left more bodies in his wake," the ME said.

It wasn't what any of them had expected—or hoped to hear. "What makes you say that?" Cassandra asked, curious. Personally, she agreed with the woman.

"The bodies all appear to have been killed during approximately the same time period," Dr. Wade answered. "No one kills this many people and then stops cold."

"He might have been arrested for another crime and imprisoned—or even killed," Cassandra suggested.

"Maybe," Danny agreed, getting into the discussion. "Or maybe he just stashed his kills elsewhere."

"Which means they could still turn up at any time," Cassandra theorized.

Danny nodded grimly. "You're probably right. They could." The New York detective was far from happy over the thought.

Neither was Travis, who shook his head as he murmured darkly to himself, "Something to look forward to."

"Hey," Cassandra said to the others, sounding cheerful, "everyone needs a reason to get out of bed in the morning."

"How about just looking forward to a good breakfast?" Travis countered.

Cassandra laughed. Travis *would* focus on food, she thought. "Leave it to you," she told her cousin, laughing.

And then she turned toward Danny. She was surprised to see that his partner, Det. Lee, had come in to join them.

She had almost forgotten about the man, she realized. The man was being exceptionally quiet. He seemed like one of those people who kept to himself and remained quiet unless he had something worthwhile to say.

Well, she had no intention of just remaining here, aging without saying a word. Cassandra was all about jumping in and getting things moving. New York might be an incredibly interesting city with a lot to offer, but at the moment, all she was interested in was being able to close the case involving her cousin and taking him home.

And right now, all she had were questions, but no answers. She needed to know just how Nathan Cavanaugh went from turning his back on his family in California to being a pile of bones that had been dug up in New York City fifteen years later.

"Do we have any kind of a last known address for Nathan or his mother?" she asked Danny. "I realize that in all probability, it can't possibly be current since they're both dead, but at least it might give us a place to start. This way, we might have a fighting chance of piecing together what Nathan did, who he did it with—and maybe, just maybe, who terminated him."

"I take it that you also buy into the story about 'Goldilocks and the Three Bears,'" Danny told her, eying her rather skeptically.

She frowned at him. She didn't appreciate being ridiculed and took offense at Danny's words. She raised her chin in defiance.

"I don't believe in fairy tales," she informed him coldly. "I do, however, believe in ruling things out, and that's what I'm attempting to do at the moment. Do you have a problem with that?"

He opened his mouth, about to answer her, then realized that maybe he was allowing the chip on his shoulder to get in the way of his thought process.

"Sorry," he finally said.

A host of different thoughts seemed to pass

through her mind. They all registered on her face as well. And then, ever so slowly, she sighed and released the breath that she had obviously been holding.

"Apology accepted. Why don't we each go back to our respective corners and start fresh?" she suggested to the New York detective.

She could see that he was considering the idea, not jumping at it one way or the other, and then finally, he nodded. "I can go along with that," he told her, agreeing.

"Do you have anywhere that we can set up and get to work, or do we have to share space with these bleached bones?" Travis asked, nodding at one of the tables.

"We were told we could use the conference room for the time being," Danny told the duo.

"Sounds good to me," Cassandra told the other man. She gestured toward the door. "Lead the way."

Danny picked up all the folders that had been put together regarding the bodies. "See you later, Doc," he said to the medical examiner.

The latter nodded, her attention already back on her work. "I'm sure it won't be long before you're here again, unfortunately," she told the gathering. "But you know where to find me if you have any questions."

With this ominous goodbye hanging over them, the detectives left.

Chapter 7

After ushering the visiting detectives into the conference room, Danny proceeded to come up with reasons to remain away from there for several hours.

It wasn't as if he didn't have anything else to do—he did. As a detective juggling cold case files, there was always more than enough for him to do.

He went to the makeshift kitchen—or corner with a small refrigerator—and pulled out small bottles of water for them. On the counter, he noticed a few packages of cookies. Maybe he should bring them too in case they needed a little pick-me-up.

Absolutely not, he told himself. What was wrong with him? Usually, he didn't think of these details, but part of him didn't want to face what was in the conference room. The idea of spending hours upon days with Cassandra Cavanaugh made him hesitate. This wasn't just a case between the two of them.

She affected him. The more time she spent with him, the more obvious it would become. Like, inevitable that their lives might wind up intertwined.

No. Just no.

Eventually, he found himself being drawn back to the conference room with its posters and notes mounted on a bulletin board, as well as the people who were apparently painstakingly going over the evidence spread out before them.

Going into the conference room was almost against his will. The detective reminded himself he was only looking in on the visiting Californians—as well as on his partner—to check if there had been any sort of progress made—or even if there was a hint of some sort of progress.

When he walked in, he had to admit that he highly doubted it. After all, not nearly enough time had gone by to even unpack the files that had been found, much less make any headway in them.

But he had to admit—albeit silently and just to himself—that he was open to any sort of pleasant surprises. There was a chance—even a slim one— that he was wrong about them. Maybe they could make the difference in solving this case.

Danny walked into the conference room, not really sure what he would find. The logical thing to expect was that the detectives were ready to call it quits for the day—if not for more than that—and maybe even go back to where they came from, because the search was leading to nothing but depressing dead ends. California detectives maybe didn't have the same work ethic that New York detectives did. An absurd notion, but of course, he had to take any potshot at them in case they screwed up everything he'd done so far with this case.

He was surprised to find that Cassandra and her cousin were all but buried in a mountain of paperwork that they were reviewing. They had painstakingly—and quickly—gone through the various notes and folders that had been compiled on the victims.

Cassandra certainly wasn't going through the same existential crisis he was. She didn't show any competitiveness toward him or his team. On the contrary, she seemed unaware of anything except the case. Maybe that was her plan.

At the moment, they were in the process of making the notes to go with them.

Danny looked at the piles of papers scattered about the table. "Did you actually find something to follow up on?" he asked incredulously, looking at Cassandra, who was seated closest to him.

"Possibly" was her vague, drawn-out response as she continued studying the notes she was reading. "The DNA identifying our cousin gives us some information to work with. The other three bodies that had been unearthed around the same time broadened the base of our scope. Based on that and the information gathered about these victims, I would say that it looks as if all four were good-looking men."

"Okay," Danny agreed expansively. "But just why would that matter one way or another?"

"Maybe it doesn't," Cassandra allowed, since she couldn't really say anything definitively—yet. "But maybe our serial killer had a vendetta against good-looking men for one reason or another, and that was why they wound up dead."

"And what would that mean?" Detective Simon Lee asked, curious as to what the California detective was thinking.

She turned toward the man, her expression appearing to be utterly guileless and an open book. "Maybe something, maybe nothing," she said expansively. "That's what we're going to have to find out."

Danny looked somewhat impressed despite himself. "And here I thought all you California types like to do is surf and work on your suntans."

"Only when there are no bodies lying around," she told him, doing her best to deadpan. She was betrayed by the appearance of what looked like a spasmodic smile that was curving the corners of her mouth.

Danny nodded, quietly kicking himself for bringing up the cliché yet again. And he didn't like that he was so self-conscious around her. She and her cousin were 100 percent focused on the case. Whatever answers they had managed to come up with, they were obviously working hard. He supposed it was time to reward that effort.

"Well, I think you guys have earned dinner. What do you think?" Danny asked, looking around the room at the detectives, including his partner seated there.

Cassandra exchanged glances with her cousin, then nodded. "I think I can be bribed," she told the lead detective agreeably.

"This is fuel for energy," Danny said. "Not a bribe."

This time, Cassandra's eyes lit up as she grinned. She was not about to argue semantics with the other detective. It certainly wasn't worth it. She would have to fight for every teasing word she said.

"Potato, po-ta-to," she replied, then told him, "Okay, we'll do it your way. However you choose to look at it, I suddenly realize that I am pretty hungry."

Danny was surprised by her admission. "I would have thought I would have had to drag that information out of you."

Her smiled only widened. "It's you New Yorkers that have to have things dragged out of them," she told him. "Not us." Cassandra spread her hands wide in an exaggerated gesture of innocence. "Our lives, in case you haven't guessed this yet, are open books." Making the declaration, she grinned and nodded toward Travis in order to include him in this dynamic as well. "There's really no point in hiding who you are, and that goes double for when you're hungry. Say it and get thee to a restaurant, fast."

Not for the first time, Danny found himself intrigued by the woman's smile. The more he looked at it, the more it seemed to draw him in with absolutely no effort exerted whatsoever.

When the thought hit him, Danny frowned. He couldn't afford to be distracted by her sea-green eyes, which looked as if they had literally been lifted straight out of tropical waters.

"Detective?" Cassandra noticed the momentary distracted look on Doyle's face. "Did I just lose you? Or do you not like hungry women?"

"Hmmm?" Her question had managed to snap him out of his mental revelry. He cleared his throat, attempting to cover up his momentary wanderings. "No, I was just temporarily distracted," he said, deliberately avoiding her eyes.

Cassandra's smile grew wider as she said, "Well, nice to know that you're human."

His expression never changed as he told her, "Hey, it's the number one requirement for joining the NYPD. Although, don't tell this to Simon Lee." He laughed out loud before realizing that they didn't really know Simon well enough to get the joke. "Some of my colleagues act like robots. That's what I meant."

Several sarcastic remarks rose to Cassandra's lips, but in the interest of the dinner that lay ahead of her, even if it turned out to be at a quickie take-out place, she decided to swallow the remarks and keep them to herself. No point in antagonizing the New York detective needlessly. She was determined to maintain a friendly front and possibly, just possibly, build some sort of a positive working relationship with the man, however temporary it might turn out to be.

Besides, she liked watching him navigate this uncomfortable relationship between them. He was doing his best, and that warmed her heart.

"I find that encouraging," she told Danny cheerfully. "So, what sort of restaurant did you have in mind?" she asked. "Takeout? Pizza? Or...?" she looked at him, her eyes widening in a silent query.

"Well, I thought pizza," he answered. "But if you'd rather have something else, maybe something fancier..." His voice trailed off, allowing her to fill the space in with a more exotic choice for dinner.

"Oh, no, no." Cassandra was quick to turn down the idea of going to some sort of a fancy restaurant. "I have heard nothing but positive things about New York pizza," she told the detective. "There's no way I'll be able to go back home once this is all wrapped up without having checked out exactly what a New York pizza has to offer that makes it supposedly superior to the kind of pizzas that we serve up within our own humble pizzerias."

Danny eyed her somewhat skeptically, wondering if she was pulling his leg or if she was actually being serious.

For now, he decided to give her the benefit of the doubt.

"Okay, get your coat, Cavanaugh. You are about to be educated," Danny said. Then, backtracking, the detective actually did the honors for her, fetching her coat and helping her with it as he stood behind her.

Cassandra's mouth all but dropped open, as she found herself completely caught off guard by the detective's manners. She hadn't pegged Detective Doyle for being such a gentlemen. Reasonably polite, yes, but definitely not an out and out gentlemen.

She had to admit that it was rather a nice discovery—and she felt a delicious shiver go down her spine. The way he could be nice to her, it seemed a bit…intimate.

Cassandra turned her head in order to look behind her, not bothering to hide her look of unabashed surprise.

As he slipped the coat onto her shoulders, he caught the expression on her face.

"What?" he asked, somewhat confused.

She didn't want to be blunt about her reaction. Clearing her throat slightly, Cassandra murmured, "Nothing, just didn't expect you to be so…helpful," she finally said, for lack of a better word.

"I take it you buy into the brash New Yorker stereotype," Danny said, guessing.

"No," Cassandra quickly denied, then retracted that assessment with a rueful expression. "Well, maybe just a little bit."

He watched her for a long moment. "Suffice to say that nobody we're dealing with is actually a one-dimensional character," the detective told her. "There are *always* extenuating circumstances."

"I'm beginning to see that." She looked around at the other detectives in the room. "So, are we all going out for pizza?" she asked, raising her voice to be heard above the noise.

Danny's partner, Simon, laughed. "Tempting though that really sounds, if I don't get home to Alice at a decent hour at least once this week, she is going to cut off my head and hand it to me, at which point, I won't be any good to anyone tomorrow—or possibly for the rest of my life," he said whimsically.

Cassandra smiled at the information the detective had just voiced. "Sounds reasonable to me," she said. "Travis?" She turned toward her cousin. "Are you going to be coming with us?" She fully expected him to say he was.

But her cousin answered by flashing a lopsided smile at her. "Well, ordinarily, I would, except that Joyce made me a really good offer that I just couldn't refuse."

"Joyce?" Cassandra repeated quizzically as she raised one bewildered eyebrow in a silent question.

Travis was more than happy to fill in the details for his cousin. "That really cute police officer who came in earlier. You know, the redhead who supplied us with all the files we currently have spread out all over the conference table. Anyway, we got to talking…" he began to confess, his voice trailing off.

"Of course you did," Cassandra said with a laugh, shaking her head. "Can't take you anywhere, can I?"

Her cousin ignored her remark and just continued with his explanation. "She told me that she knew of this really great out-of-the-way place that most people don't even frequent. They just drive right past it," Travis said. "To quote Joyce, 'The food is to die for,'" her cousin added with a wide grin.

Cassandra regarded him with a slight show of concern. She wasn't thrilled with his choice of words, not after what they had discovered happened to Nathan all those years ago.

"Just make sure that you don't," Cassandra cautioned.

"Hey, Cass," Travis answered, amused. "I'm touched." He dramatically placed his hand over his heart. "But I can take care of myself. Trust me," he said with a wink.

This case was getting to her. This was the first time that the family had lost someone to murder, and she had to admit that that did make her feel more than just a little bit vulnerable.

"I know you can," she told him, "but just in case, don't forget to be aware of your surroundings."

"Yes, ma'am," Travis replied solemnly, giving her a smart military salute.

At that moment, a rather pretty young officer

looked into the conference room. Her eyes instantly met Travis's.

"Ready?" the redhead asked brightly, obviously eager to leave the conference room and get rolling.

"Absolutely," Cassandra's cousin replied. "See you in the morning, Cass." He nodded at her, then turned his attention toward Doyle. "Detective," he said, nodding at the man.

With that, Cassandra's cousin walked out of the room, allowing the attractive officer to lead the way.

The conference room had emptied rather quickly, Cassandra noted.

Danny had turned toward Cassandra. "Guess that just leaves us," he said. "Unless you'd just rather go straight to your hotel room and go to bed," he suggested.

Cassandra blinked. "Excuse me?" she asked, looking at the detective as if the latter had just slipped into some sort of a foreign language.

Danny suddenly realized what the woman from California thought he was saying to her. His skin went hot from the mere suggestion. He definitely wasn't thinking straight. "I meant to get some sleep, not anything else."

Indignant, Cassandra tossed her head slightly, sending her straight blond hair flying over her shoulder. "I know that," she informed him crisply.

"Good," Danny replied. "Because if I was tempted to say anything else to you," the detective told her,

"I guarantee that you would definitely know it. Now then, are you ready?"

"Absolutely," she announced.

Danny shut off the light in the conference room. Following him, Cassandra raised the back of her collar as they went toward the elevator.

Because it was dark and growing colder by the moment, once they were outside, Danny decided that although the restaurant he had in mind wasn't all that far away, they would be better served if he drove there rather than just walk.

"Walking there would probably be faster," Danny told her. "But definitely not warmer, so we're taking my car," he told her, bringing her over to the parked vehicle.

Cassandra obligingly slid into the passenger seat, doing her best to try to warm up.

"I'd turn up the heat," Danny offered once she was in the car. "But by the time it finally kicked in and did its job, we'll be at the restaurant," he told her. "But finding parking might take a little longer."

She was doing her best to huddle into herself and attempt to keep warm. Complaining about how she felt was not her style. But she had to admit that this New York weather certainly made her miss Southern California.

Cassandra had no intentions of commenting on how cold she felt. "You know best," she told him agreeably, doing her best to be positive.

One would have thought that skyscrapers would keep out the cold, but instead, the wind whipped against the buildings and onto unsuspecting humans trying to navigate this efficient city. One gust had almost knocked her over just before she'd gotten into his car.

"It's nice the department has such convenient parking," she commented. Her teeth were still chattering.

"One of the few perks, making sure the car is ready to go."

Danny took a corner, coasting to a stop as the light changed. He turned and smiled at her. "You're nicer when we're not reviewing information that has to do with the work of a serial killer and the guy's victims," he commented.

"Hey, cracking wise helps to keep me sane," she told the detective. Her hands started to warm up.

Danny nodded. "I can definitely see the need for that," he told her agreeably.

There was a great deal of traffic in the streets, he noted. So, what else was new? One had to learn to maintain serenity in Manhattan traffic and pad at least thirty minutes into travel time. Danny weaved his way toward the restaurant he had selected, the one he tended to frequent whenever he wanted to sample a really excellent slice of pizza.

The great part about living in the city was finding these gems hidden in neighborhoods far away from work. About twenty blocks from the squad room was his favorite haven, where he'd spent many a frustrating evening poring over case details and enjoying pizza and a cannoli or two.

Within moments, Danny pulled his vehicle up in front of the very small space directly in front of the compact pizza restaurant. As he stepped out of the car, he realized that this might have been the only time he'd brought someone to his special place. For the first time, the cold hit him hard.

Chapter 8

The aroma, once they walked into the restaurant, was absolute heaven. The moment Cassandra took a deep breath, her stomach instantly responded.

She hadn't realized that she was *this* hungry until now.

If the pizza tasted half as good as it smelled, she was very glad that the detective had offered to bring her here. She could get good food in Aurora, but she had the feeling New York pizza would be an extra special experience, especially with Detective Doyle.

The restaurant's finished mahogany interior was modest with maps and prints supporting all things Italian, especially food. Cassandra admired drawings of celebrities who had visited the establishment. There was nothing glitzy about this place, but it seemed well loved.

"Uncle Andrew would just love this place," she commented to the detective as the aroma seemed to continue to swirl around her, teasing her appetite.

The moment they were shown to their table and took their seats, Danny pushed the menu toward her. He knew the selection by heart and already knew what he was going to order.

"Uncle Andrew?" the detective questioned.

"Sorry," Cassandra apologized. She realized that the detective undoubtedly didn't have a clue who she was talking about. "I have a tendency to think that people know who I'm talking about when I'm making references to members of my family," she said to the detective. Taking a breath, she proceeded to launch into an explanation and to enlighten the man. "Aside from being the family patriarch, Andrew Cavanaugh was once the chief of the Aurora Police Department."

"What happened?" Danny asked her. "Did he get voted out?" He would have assumed that had to be the logical answer. Just then, he saw the waitress pass by and raised his hand to catch her attention. Seeing him, the woman held her hand up, indicating that she would be there shortly.

"No." Cassandra shot down the detective's logical conclusion to fill him in on what actually happened. "Uncle Andrew's wife disappeared one evening after they had had a rare argument. When she didn't come home, he went looking for her. That was when he discovered that it appeared her car had gone over the side of the road and right into the river, washing downstream.

"When all attempts at finding Rose wound up failing, Uncle Andrew was forced to resign and take an early retirement. He had five kids to take care of, not all of whom were grown yet. Eventually, he fell back on the occupation that had seen him through his college days."

"Which was?" Danny asked as the waitress finally approached their tiny table.

"Cooking," Cassandra told the detective brightly.

The dark-haired young woman stopped at their table and flashed a warm smile at them. "What can I get for you folks?"

Cassandra gestured toward the detective. "I think you have a better idea of the kind of things that they serve here that really taste excellent," she told the detective as she put down her menu. "I'll let you make the selection for me."

Danny didn't seem all that sure about the matter. A lot of people could be very fussy about what they ate. "Are you sure about this?"

Cassandra never hesitated. "Absolutely. And remember, serial killers make me hungry, so no need to get me just a big salad."

Danny caught himself laughing at her declaration. "Wow, serial killers make you hungry. First time I ever heard of that being used as an excuse," he told the visiting detective. "For me, killers tend to kill my appetite. Don't know why I'm hungry now."

Her eyes sparkled as she grinned up at the detective. "Guess there's a first time for everything," Cassandra told him.

Danny placed their dinner order, then handed the menus back to the waitress. "Guess so."

She waited until the waitress retreated, then turned toward the detective. "I'm kind of curious," Cassandra began.

Danny blew out a breath. "Now there's a surprise," he commented, hints of amusement in his eyes.

"I'll ignore that," she told him, then continued, saying, "I know why I'm in this insane business. This is all that I've ever wanted to be since I was a little girl, but why did you get mixed up in it? Did you feel it was a calling, or was this the only thing open that you felt you could sign up for at the time?" Cassandra cocked her head, waiting for his answer.

Danny frowned at her. He felt as if he had been put on the spot. "You're awfully nosy, you know that?"

She lifted her shoulders in a careless gesture, then let them drop. "I guess you could say that being nosy is all part of the family business," Cassandra said. "But that still really doesn't get you out of answering my question."

He didn't understand why the woman was asking these questions. "I thought you said that you knew all about me," he reminded her, referring to their earlier conversation.

"I'm not talking about the intimate, important stuff," she admitted. "I mean, why do you do what you do? And don't tell me it's for the pay, because I know better," she told him. "You could earn a lot more in another line of work."

Danny frowned at the woman sitting across from him. He hated baring his soul, it just wasn't his way. But then, maybe he owed it to his aunt to have this story finally come out and see the light of day.

He was about to begin talking, but at that moment, their perky waitress returned with their extra large pepperoni pizza. She placed the tray on the table between the two of them, then moved back.

"Will there be anything else, sir?" the young woman asked.

"Not right now," he told her. "I'll let you know if there is."

The waitress nodded. Danny waited until she withdrew before he finally continued answering Cassandra's question.

For a long moment, he stared at his serving, looking for the right words. Remembering this part of his life was not easy for him.

Finally he told her, "My Aunt Gina was killed by a serial killer."

Her eyes widened. She hadn't been expecting that. For a second, the detective had managed to steal her breath from her.

Cassandra reached across the table, surprising the detective by covering his hand with her own. "Oh, Doyle, I'm so very sorry to hear that. Did you ever catch the guy?" Because she had such faith in him, she fully expected the detective to tell her that he had. So, when he shook his head, admitting that he hadn't, she found herself doubly stunned. "That must have been so hard for you. I'm *really* sorry," she told him in all sincerity.

The pizza, as gorgeous as it was, sat between them untouched. At least for now. Instinctively, Danny wanted to change the subject, but that would have been too awkward. Plus, something about Cassandra made him want to confide in her.

But the failure in Aunt Gina's case still gnawed at him. He tried to shrug off his inability to find his aunt's killer. "Hey, this isn't like the movies," he told her. "This is to remind me that despite all the work that's put in, sometimes things just don't have a way of working themselves out. What this did," he told the California detective, "was make me even more determined to capture killers and bring them to justice whenever possible."

She nodded. "I totally understand," Cassandra said. "Just don't forget to take two breaths in quick succession."

He looked at her, rather astonished. "You're giving me tips?"

"Just trying to be helpful." She paused. She just had to ask. "Were you and your aunt close?"

He stared off into the distance. "She was family." He pressed his lips together, remembering things he was not about to say out loud. "One day she was there, the next, she wasn't." He looked rather saddened by the recollection. "She was a nice lady. Kind of close to my age," he recalled. "The day that it happened, it hit my mother really hard. She had practically raised Aunt Gina, who was a lot younger than she was." He sighed to himself, unaware that the sound carried over to Cassandra. "One day she just never came home from school."

Cassandra nodded, taking it all in. And then she asked, "Are you still keeping notes on her disappearance?"

He stared at the woman sitting across from him, surprised that she would ask something so intuitive. "How did you know?"

Cassandra's smile widened. "We're not all that different, you and I," she told him. Finally turning her attention to the pizza, she took a bite and the moment she did, her eyes all but lit up as she smiled broadly.

Cassandra nodded at her plate. "This tastes really fantastic."

Danny was pleased by her response. "Did you think I was making it up?" he asked her incredulously.

"No," she denied, then went on to say, "but, well, I thought that maybe you were exaggerating just a little." Cassandra held up her thumb and forefinger to create a tiny space.

"I never exaggerate," he told her. "The consequences for that sort of thing are just way too great. You get caught in an exaggeration, and when that comes to light, nobody ever believes you again."

"Can't argue with that," she agreed.

"Oh sure you can," he told her. He had the impression that the woman could argue the fur off a cat.

Between the two of them, the pizza disappeared quickly. Before she knew it, the slices were gone, and she found herself staring at an empty pizza dish.

Danny saw the way she was eying the tray. "Would you like me to order more?"

"Yes," she answered with feeling. "But I'll have to pass on that. Otherwise, I'm really going to explode."

"No, you wouldn't," he contradicted.

She laughed. "If I were you, I wouldn't bet the family farm on that. Or stand too close," she warned.

He knew she wasn't about to explode, but he decided to keep that to himself. There was no point in getting into any sort of a dispute with her. He was just grateful that she'd gotten off the subject of his aunt's killer. Discussing personal matters took him out of his comfort zone. Everything about Cassandra took him out of his comfort zone. If they focused on pizza and the case, everything would be okay.

Looking at her empty plate, he did ask, "Can I get you anything else?"

But Cassandra shook her head. "Oh, no, I really am *more* than full," she told him. Her eyes crinkled as she smiled at the detective. "That had to be the best pizza I've ever had, bar none."

"Glad you feel that way." It was time to call it a night, he thought. "Can I take you to the hotel?"

"You don't have to go out of your way and do that," she told him. "I can definitely walk to the hotel. It's not all that far away."

To Cassandra's surprise, the detective shook his head. "Sorry, but you're much too attractive to walk that distance in the dark. Things have changed around here lately, and as long as I'm responsible for you, I'm not about to take any chances."

She actually was safe to walk around at night by herself, but he still wanted to keep an eye on her. Part of his job was to protect others, and he took that seriously. Plus, she wasn't a New Yorker. How ungentlemanly he'd be if he just let her go to the hotel by herself.

Still seated at the small table for two, she looked up at the detective. "When did you become responsible for me?"

"Since you and your cousin walked into my department to help work on my cold cases," he told her. Taking out his wallet, he peeled off a couple of twenties and left them on the table to pay for the meal and leave a healthy tip for the waitress.

"Ready to go?" he asked her as he rose to his feet. For a moment, she felt like arguing with him over his intention to drive her to her hotel, but what was the point? It would only ruin what had been, up until now, a very enjoyable evening. So she agreed to what he had said.

"Sure," she told him. "Let's go."

Danny paused to help Cassandra with her coat. She twisted around to look at him. Once again, surprise registered on her face.

"Why do you look so surprised?" he asked. After all, he had helped her on with her coat once already.

"I thought maybe you grew tired of being the gentleman," she told him, nodding at the coat on her shoulders.

"You don't think all that much of me, do you?" he asked.

"No, it's not that," she said as they walked out of the restaurant and over to where he parked his vehicle. "I've just learned that despite everything, I just should never take anything for granted—no matter how much I might be tempted to do just that."

Reaching his car, she paused as he opened the door for her. A really cold breeze had picked up, sending an even colder chill up and down her body.

She did her best not to shiver.

Closing the door behind her, Danny got in on the other side of the vehicle. He noted the look on her face. The cold made her really uncomfortable. He could tell by her apparent stiffness. Her features seemed closed off, focusing on the sudden drop in temperature. Sometimes, it even took his breath away.

"I bet you can't wait to get back to sunny California," Danny commented.

"We have our cold days," she told him. "Not like this, of course." She had to agree. "But it can get pretty cold in Southern California."

The detective truly doubted it, but for now, he just went along with what she said for the sake of not getting into an argument.

"If you say so," Danny told her. He started up his vehicle, then looked in her direction. "What hotel are you staying in?"

She rattled off the name of the hotel, then started to give him directions. She stopped when he began to laugh.

Cassandra looked at him quizzically.

"I've lived here all my life," he told her. "I know where the hotel is. I know every subway station, street, rodent, bodega, park…"

"You did not just say rodent, did you?"

Danny chuckled. "I sure did. Before you leave, we're going to take the subway. You'll see the finer things in this great city."

"You're trying to scare me," Cassandra said.

"Is that even possible?"

Cassandra folded her arms. He was really trying to get to her, and no way could he uncover her very minor fear of small living things…like rats. "No, we have our own special creatures in California."

"Well, there's nothing like a New York subway rat looking for its dinner."

"You can stop talking about rats now, Detective Doyle."

They both laughed and then paused as Danny drove the few blocks to Cassandra's hotel. He pulled up to the front and parked the vehicle in front of the revolving door. "Here you go, door to door service," he announced. "I'll be by tomorrow morning to pick you and your cousin up. Eight o'clock all right with you?"

She thought about her cousin. Travis would be all right with it, she decided. "Eight o'clock will be fine."

And then Cassandra proceeded to completely surprise Danny by leaning in and brushing a kiss against his lips. She didn't know what had gotten into her, but it seemed a natural way to end the night. Plus, the urge had overpowered her. The second her lips touched his, she felt a giddiness that had been building all day long. She'd needed this kiss, wanted it for herself and for him. It didn't seem likely that he'd had enough California sunshine in his life.

"Thank you for the pizza," she said, drawing her head back, and then, with that, she got out of the car and closed the door behind her.

She left him utterly stunned, staring after her as she quickly hurried up to the hotel and then made her way to the revolving door.

Pushing against it, she proceeded to disappear into the interior of the hotel.

The detective continued staring at the hotel's interior, doing his best to attempt to recover. What the hell had just happened?

Yesterday, all he'd seen were the details of this case, and now, this detective from the other coast had kissed him. A lot could change in a day.

Not to mention, he could feel her lips on his long after the moment had faded.

The word *Wow* continued to echo in his head even after she had disappeared into the hotel.

Part of him couldn't wait for tomorrow to come. The other part was deeply afraid. Afraid he couldn't control this new element in his life.

Chapter 9

Rather than go to bed and get some much-needed sleep, Cassandra decided to try to piece together the last few days of her late cousin's life. Was Nathan killed by someone he just happen to stumble across, and it was just a murder of convenience? Or did the killer target Nathan on purpose?

Maybe, for lack of a better motive, it had been someone who was jealous of Nathan and had decided to kill him for some reason known only to the killer.

It was definitely a puzzle, Cassandra thought, frustrated.

She decided to make a list to send to Valri. Her cousin was an ace when it came to anything related to technology. Her searches were famous, and Cassandra felt confident that Valri could make heads or tails out of the situation. Because of the hour—and in deference to the fact that Valri did have a home life, rather than call her computer wizard of a cousin, she decided to text.

Cassandra included a homey greeting along with her question.

New York is every bit as busy as its reputation makes it out to be, and Nathan's life remains as big a mystery as you might think. If it's not too much trouble, could you possibly trace his last steps before he met his untimely end? Nobody here in the city is as great as you are at unearthing hidden facts.

By the way, Travis says hi!

Travis, of course, had no idea she was texting Valri, but she thought it was a nice touch to include him in the missive. It made for a united front.

Crossing her fingers, Cassandra sent the text.

After placing her cell phone next to her bed, she switched off the light and finally lay down. She stifled a yawn, waiting to fall asleep. For some reason, her body wouldn't relax. Perhaps it was the city's energy surging through her. They didn't call it the city that never sleeps for nothing. Maybe it was the case or even a touch of jet lag. There was a three-hour difference, which actually did make a difference.

Sadly, sleep came in small snatches and whenever she would wake up, it was as if she hadn't closed her eyes at all.

This case was getting to her, she thought. There was no other explanation for the restlessness that had taken over her body.

Exhausted and sleepy because of her highly in-grained sense of duty, Cassandra was still up, so she showered and dressed before dawn. She took a quick peek out her window, then shut the shades again. It still looked pretty cold outside, with thick gray clouds covering the city.

She fully intended to make her way downstairs, grab a cup of coffee in the hotel café and get to the precinct before Danny had a chance to come by and pick her up.

It was against her better nature to be indebted to anyone, even to someone who was as good-looking as Detective Danny Doyle. She hadn't been raised that way, she thought as she collected her cell phone and her laptop. Putting both items into her backpack, she zipped it up, then grabbed her winter coat.

She had just slipped it on and was about to leave her hotel room when she heard a knock on her door.

Habit had her placing her hand on the weapon in her pocket before she went to the door. She kept the chain in place as she cautiously asked, "Who is it?"

"Rudolph. Santa's reindeer," the voice on the other side of the door answered. "I got lost."

Instantly recognizing the voice, Cassandra glanced at her watch. Danny. Didn't this guy ever sleep? He was worse than she was.

"Danny?" Cassandra asked just to be certain her imagination wasn't playing tricks on her.

"Very good," he commended her. "What gave me away?"

She laughed. "Nobody I met here so far sounds as grumpy as you do," she told him.

"You're turning my head with your flattery," he told her sarcastically. "C'mon, Cassandra, open the door before someone phones the front desk and complains about being disturbed by the sound of raised voices."

In response to his instruction, he heard the locks being clicked open. Within less than a minute, he found himself gazing at the startlingly awake California detective.

"Why are you here?" she asked.

He made a guess as to what had prompted her to ask that since they had agreed to his coming by to pick her and her cousin up last night. "Is it too early for you?"

In response, Cassandra spread out her hands to indicate that not only was she up, but she was dressed and about to leave the room.

"No," she said. "But I would have thought you wouldn't want to miss out on getting a little extra sleep yourself."

"Oh, but I did," Danny told her innocently.

Her brow furrowed. Right, like she believed that.

"Do you New Yorkers measure sleep by the thimbleful?" she asked him. "Because I figure that you didn't get any kind of decent sleep at all."

"It's not how much sleep you get, it's the kind of sleep you manage to log in," Danny said.

He actually sounded as if he believed that, she thought. Cassandra looked at him skeptically. "Meaning?"

"Meaning I'm ready to get back to work if you are—or I can just leave you here and come back later," he told her.

Oh, no, he wasn't about to treat her as if she were some sort of frail princess. She was here for a reason, and she intended to fulfill that reason, she thought.

"Now will be fine," Cassandra assured him. "You know," she told him, "I'm not used to having someone hovering over me, acting like he's waiting for me to cave in on myself."

"I am not hovering," he said. "I'm *watching over* you. There is a difference," he assured her. "Do you have any way of knowing if your cousin is ready yet? I can take him to the precinct as well."

"I'm sure he would appreciate it, although I don't know if he's awake yet. It's three hours earlier in California. Working this case—all of it—is rather exhausting, and I have no idea what time he turned in last night." A smile played on her lips. "Or if he even turned in. The last I heard, he was having a late dinner with that policewoman who picked him up."

Travis was a charmer, for sure. It wouldn't be out of character for him to be still on his date. But she also knew that it wasn't a good idea to wake him out of a sound sleep. Her cousin could catch up to them later.

"Why don't you call his room? If he doesn't pick up, just leave him a message," the detective suggested. "As you pointed out, your cousin can take care of himself."

"What I pointed out is that my cousin and *I* can take care of ourselves. I was the primary person in that sentence," Cassandra said quickly.

Danny pretended not to hear that part of it. "Why don't you give your cousin a call and ask him if he wants a ride?"

Frowning at him, she proceeded to dial Travis's cell phone. Mentally, she counted off the number of rings she heard on the other end and was about to hang up after she got to six, but she suddenly heard the line pick up.

Travis's incredibly sleepy voice barked a barely audible "Hello?" in Cassandra's ear.

"So, you are alive," she said, feigning surprise.

Her cousin sighed deeply into her ear. "And so, apparently, are you. You're a terrible person to call me this early." He yawned, trying to pull himself together. "Didn't Uncle Angus teach you anything about knowing how important it is to get a decent night's sleep?"

She turned away so that Danny couldn't overhear her. "No, he was too busy stressing doing a decent job. His favorite saying was always, 'It ain't over until it's over,' and these bodies that were discovered tell us that this is definitely *not* over.

"I called Valri and gave her all the information we had. Hopefully, we can recreate Nathan's last known movements. Maybe that'll help us find out who the other people were who were buried with him—and how they all wound up getting there."

Travis yawned in her ear again. She knew that meant he was getting up and coming to. "Has she gotten back to you yet?" her cousin asked.

She could only laugh in response. She was very aware that Danny gave her a curious look. "Valri's fast, but she's not superhuman, Travis. Besides, I just left her that message late last night. We'll hear from her," she told her cousin confidently. "Now get dressed. Detective Doyle has graciously volunteered to bring us back to the police station."

She couldn't read the detective's expression at the moment, but she could guess that it probably had something to do with the last thing that had gone down last night.

She had kissed Danny last night. It was an impulse, and the last thing she wanted was for him to think that was an open invitation on her part. When it came to the detective, she definitely liked what she saw, but she didn't want him believing that she was throwing herself at him.

At least, not until she knew how he felt about her. This wasn't about insecurity. . But...he moved her. More than that. He'd shaken her in a way she hadn't felt. She saw deep into him, the way he carried himself and went about his case, his life.

He needed someone like her. Not only did she share

his passion for the job, but she also liked how being with him stopped time—in the best possible way.

"So?" Danny asked Cassandra the second she terminated the call and closed her phone.

"He'll be here in ten minutes," she told the detective, knowing how her cousin operated.

Danny looked unconvinced. "We'll see."

Suddenly, they were truly alone together with what happened the night before. What could possibly go wrong?

As it turned out, Travis was not ready in ten minutes. He was ready in eleven.

Danny glanced at the detective from Southern California. "You people are freakishly on time," he couldn't help commenting. "It's very strange. I was thinking maybe an hour, two tops before he'd be ready."

She grinned at him. "Told you." As Travis walked into the hotel room, she pushed a container of coffee into his hand. "I took the liberty of getting your coffee for you. Drink up and let's go." With that, she turned on her heel and led the way out.

Danny looked at the woman's cousin. "Has she always been this bossy?" he asked as he followed Travis out.

Travis laughed. "From the first moment she opened her eyes—not in the morning but *ever,*" he emphasized. "My theory is that Cass hears music from an entirely different drummer and just marches to it."

Getting on the elevator, she turned toward the two men who got on behind her. Danny pressed the down button. "You do realize that I'm right here and can hear every word you're saying, right?" she asked as she looked at the two men.

"Never doubted it for a moment," Danny told her.

Reaching the ground floor, they stepped off the elevator. The moment they did, Cassandra's phone began to ring. Mentally crossing her fingers for good news, she took her cell out and held it to her ear.

"This is Detective Cavanaugh."

"Apparently, I don't even get a break when you go away, do I?"

The second Cassandra heard Valri's voice, she immediately drew her shoulders back a little.

"I'm afraid that's what you get for being the best, Valri. Your reputation has spread far and wide."

"Yeah, yeah. I also know what else is being spread," Valri told her cousin. She could just see Cassandra rolling her eyes. Time to get down to business. "I don't have anything for you yet, but I'll get back to you the second that I do," Valri promised her.

"I'm going to hold you to that," Cassandra promised. "Talk to you later," she said, concluding the conversation. Cassandra tucked her phone away into her coat pocket, leaving it within accessible reach. "Valri said she'd get back to us," she told both men.

It was Danny who nodded. "I heard. How good is this Valri person at keeping her word? I mean, all she did was call you to say she's going to call you later. Isn't that like having a meeting about meetings?"

Travis smothered a laugh.

"Well, aren't you a funny guy with your New York sense of humor? It's called communication, fella. And Valri is better than anyone you've ever met," Cassandra told him with conviction. "Besides, Valri knows that I'll haunt her until I get an answer," she said with a grin. "Let's call it a preemptive strike."

Danny laughed. "I can totally believe that." Walking out of the hotel, the detective led the way to where he had parked his vehicle. He had actually found a space and congratulated himself about it.

He waited until Cassandra got into the passenger seat and Travis climbed into the back seat behind him.

The detective was about to start up the police vehicle when his cell phone rang.

Now what? he couldn't help wondering.

"Doyle," he announced as he opened his phone and put it against his ear.

Whatever else he was about to say died on his lips as he listened to what the person on the other end had to tell him.

Looking at the expression on his face, Cassandra couldn't begin to guess what he was being told. Something was obviously wrong. She did her best to piece things together from listening to his side of the conversation.

"When?" Danny demanded. His next question

was, "How many? Are you sure?" That was followed up with a very deep sigh. "We'll be right there," he told the person on the other end of his phone call. "We're just leaving the hotel now."

With that, he closed his cell phone and slipped it back into his pocket.

Cassandra waited as long as she could without jumping out of her skin. The moment the detective stopped talking, she asked, "We'll be right where?"

"They found more bodies. This time, they were on the other end of the construction site," he told the two people in his car.

Travis leaned over toward the detective. "How many more bodies?" he wanted to know.

"Hard to tell," Detective Doyle answered honestly. "They just found the different body parts. According to what dispatch just told me, there were a whole bunch of body parts, not nearly as well preserved as the ones that were initially found. Whoever did this dismantling was not nearly as careful about preserving these parts as the other ones were. The killer was either in a hurry—or he didn't care nearly as much as he had earlier."

Travis hazarded a guess. "Maybe it's not the same person."

"Oh, it's the same person all right," Danny assured the other two detectives. There was no missing the conviction in his voice.

"What makes you so sure?" Cassandra asked.

"Because the killer carved what looked like initials into the bones. We need to have the pathologist examine them and draw whatever conclusions he can from them. The letters are hard to make out—but they are definitely letters," Danny said, assuring them.

Cassandra frowned. This could all be a tempest in a teapot. "What if the serial killer is dead by now?"

"It is a possibility," Danny agreed, then countered, "But what if he isn't? What if this turns out to be just another wave in this guy's killing spree? After all, until those first group of bones turned up, we didn't even realize that we were dealing with a serial killer."

"All the more reason for us to get some answers. The faster we get those answers, the better," Cassandra said with conviction. She looked at Danny. "All right, let's get going," she urged.

"Yes, ma'am," he murmured, pretending to be docile as he started up his vehicle.

Chapter 10

"Doesn't take long for word to get around, does it?" Travis asked, looking out of the police car window at the crowds that were gathering on either side of the newly cleared construction site off the West Side Highway. Because of the isolated nature of this site, it was the perfect place to dump bodies, especially with construction happening. Someone was bound to find the gore and invite others to the party.

"People have a macabre sense of curiosity, I guess," Danny commented. He pulled his vehicle to stop as close to the scene as he could get.

Cassandra spoke up. "Not me," she said with feeling. "I don't get why anyone would want to get up close to human suffering."

Danny looked at her, highly skeptical of the sentiment that the sexy California detective had just expressed.

"You're not curious?" he said. It was obvious that he didn't believe her. To him, curiosity was the very foundation of being a decent detective.

"No, not in the usual way. I just want this case to be closed and over. But I have to admit that I have this sick feeling this predator is going to keep on killing people until we catch him."

"Men," Danny said with emphasis. "This serial killer is going to keep on killing *men* until we catch him."

Danny had gotten Travis's attention. Up until this point, that idea hadn't occurred to either him or to his cousin. "You think this guy is motivated by some sort of feelings of jealousy?" Travis asked as he got out of the vehicle right behind Danny and his cousin.

"If I had to make a guess," Cassandra added, "I'd say that maybe it's more of a feeling of inadequacy than just jealousy," the California detective speculated.

"Why?" Danny said, challenging her thought process. Since the time he was twelve years old, he took nothing at face value.

She shrugged. "Why not?" she challenged. "There are an awful lot of possibilities here," she told the two detectives as the three of them walked over to the newly discovered burial site. "We just have to examine every one of them."

Cassandra shifted over to the side and then abruptly

stopped walking as something on the ground caught her eye. "Hey, guys, I think I found something," she announced.

"Just one something?" Danny asked. There seemed to be bones spread out everywhere he looked. It had to mean three, possibly four more bodies.

But Cassandra had taken out her cell phone and was crouching over what appeared to be the bones, taking pictures. Closer examination indicated that there was a class ring on the ground.

Satisfied that she had captured the ring that had seemingly fallen off a finger by accident, she pulled out a handkerchief from her pocket and used that to pick it up.

Travis was looking over her shoulder. "Think that belongs to our killer?" he asked.

"Well, it's a man's university ring. That's about all I can see at the moment," Cassandra said. "You might be able to pull prints off it—if there are any— or find some kind of number inside, depending on the metal."

Danny was right next to her. "We can send it to our lab," he told the other two detectives. "See if we can find out who it belongs to."

Keeping it tucked into the handkerchief, Cassandra handed the ring over to Danny. "Could have belonged to the killer—or one of the victims," she said, theorizing as various ideas popped into her head, crowding one another out. "If they can lift a print," she said, watching Danny carefully tuck the ring away, "Maybe that'll get us closer to some sort of an answer."

"Maybe," Danny said, although he didn't sound very hopeful or convinced of the possibility. It was obvious that he didn't allow himself to get carried away until he could actually prove something.

"Hey, every little bit helps," Cassandra told the detective with unabashed conviction. "You've got to maintain positive thoughts," she said to both men. But it was obvious that she was really talking to the New York detective.

Danny shot a glance at the man next to him. "How does she stay so upbeat all the time?" he asked, then lowered his voice just a little. "Is she on something?"

"Just terminal optimism," Travis told him. "It's a requirement if you're a Cavanaugh. At least for most of us."

Danny read between the lines. "You mean there are a few of you that *aren't* so terribly chipper?" he asked.

Overhearing the detective, Cassandra added in her two cents. "One or two," she told the New York detective. For a moment, she pretended to be serious. "But we don't talk about them." She grinned at Danny. "We're waiting for them to come around and be like the rest of us." And then she turned serious. "In my opinion, I think that your forensic examiners should see if they can make any sort of identifications or if there's a way to compare these bones to your missing persons files from around that time."

Cassandra took in a long breath as she looked around the grounds, taking in the milling policemen and women. "We just need something to steer us in the right direction. I've got this gut feeling that these bodies are all connected in some fashion. We just need to identify one person, and that just might provide us with the key to all the others."

"You really think so?" Danny asked. He had the same skepticism in his voice as he'd had previously.

Cassandra shrugged her shoulders. It wasn't a helpless gesture; it was one open to suggestions. "There's nothing else on the table right now, we might as well give this idea a try." She saw the dismissive look on Doyle's face, which caused her to bring up a point. "If I recall correctly, the Son of Sam was finally caught because of a parking ticket. You just never know where your break might come from," she said. She shifted over to the side as Danny's people carefully loaded the newly discovered bones into a truck for transportation. They were on their way back to the precinct to work on assembling this latest jigsaw puzzle.

He blew out a breath as he looked at the support team that had been assigned to him and this case.

"You heard the lady," he told the staff. "Let's get this back to the precinct. We've got work to do, people."

Danny had some of his people focusing on reconstructing the scattered bones into a whole skeletal structure and another team combing through the missing persons reports, pulling those that had to do with missing men of a certain age.

He was convinced that Cassandra was onto something. Or if for some reason she wasn't, then it was up to him to find a way to disprove it.

Cassandra and Travis volunteered to be part of the team reviewing the missing person's files.

The piles of papers they were going through had been narrowed down to include good-looking males between the ages of eighteen and forty. It seemed like as good a place to start as any, he reasoned. That idea hadn't been explored yet, and who knew? It might just work.

It was getting late, and one by one, most of the people had left the department for the day. Danny was growing bleary-eyed as he looked at the face in the file that Cassandra had just pulled and brought over to him.

"You think he's good-looking?" Danny asked her. His tone told her that he didn't harbor those thoughts himself.

She glanced at the photo in the file. "Well, he's not about to stop any clocks, if that's what you're asking." She smiled at him as she placed the information in a small, growing pile. "Besides, beauty is in the eye of the beholder. I can see another man being jealous of him," she told Danny. "Our serial killer might easily see this guy as being competition, one way or another."

Danny picked up the photo and studied it for a moment. The skepticism in his eyes grew. "One way or another?" he echoed, then looked up at the woman. "Just what is that supposed to mean?" he wanted to know.

"Competition when it came to the ladies—or to another man," she said expansively.

Danny rolled his eyes. He didn't see it that way. "If you say so," he said, his voice trailing off without any sort of emphasis behind it.

Danny's tone had caught her attention.

They were the last two people left in the conference room. Everyone else had already gone for the night. That included Travis, right after he had made Cassandra promise to either have Danny bring her to her room or to have her take an Uber as a last resort.

At the time when Travis had made his request, Cassandra had waved her cousin off, telling him that he worried too much and that she was perfectly capable of taking care of herself. That was when her cousin had turned toward Doyle, who needed no prompting.

"I'll see she gets to the hotel all right," Danny promised.

It was obvious that Travis didn't trust his cousin to go along with this. Travis stifled a yawn as he looked at Cassandra. "I can stay," he told them.

"Go!" both Cassandra and Danny ordered in unison. Exhausted, Travis nodded as he stifled another yawn.

"I'll be back first thing in the morning," he promised, making his way toward the door and out of the conference room.

"And then there were two," Cassandra murmured under her breath as she heard the door close behind her cousin.

Danny made no response. He was busy reading the latest missing persons folder he had pulled over in front of him. Something within what he had read struck him. He had almost missed it on his first pass, but then he reread the passage.

"Hmm," he commented to himself.

Cassandra's attention was immediately aroused. Blinking, she looked up. "'Hmmm,'?" she repeated quizzically. "Did you find something, Detective?"

"It's probably nothing," he told her, dismissing his first reaction.

"But…?" she prompted, waiting for him to fill in the blank. When he didn't say anything, she pressed the point. "You never told me you were a tease."

That caught his attention. "A tease?" the detective repeated.

"Yes, you threw a statement out there, then didn't follow it up," she told him.

He frowned at her. "I'd say that you were the tease, not me."

"I'm just trying to gather all the information I can on these cases so we can finally catch a break and hopefully finally catch this guy before he strikes again."

Danny listened to what she was saying, then slowly nodded. The woman had a point. "You know, you really would be a very good addition to my team," he told her. This time, Danny allowed a drop of his admiration to slip through.

"*Your* team?" she repeated, surprised that he would say something like that to her.

"Well, it is my team," he reminded her. "And if you must know, you've displayed more enthusiasm for attempting to solve a crime than I've witnessed in a very long time. Ever think about staying and working in New York?" he asked.

She paused for a moment, looking at him. The man was actually being serious, she thought. "Now don't take this the wrong way," she began slowly, "but no. New York is a great place to visit, but I really couldn't live the rest of my life here," Cassandra told him.

His perfectly shaped eyebrows rose just a bit. "Mind if I ask why?"

She knew he was taking this to heart—which surprised her—but she had to be honest with him. Cassandra began to review her reasons.

"The heat in the summer, the cold in the winter, and I hear that you have very hungry mosquitoes that like to go to town, munching on people. I can go on," she said.

"No, that's not necessary," he told her. Danny shut her down. "I see you've given this a lot of thought."

"Actually, those were the first things that came to mind," she told the detective in all honesty. Just then, her stomach rumbled rather loudly. Cassandra flushed. "Sorry."

Danny immediately realized what the problem was. "No, I'm the one who should apologize," he told her. "I had all of you working straight through the late afternoon when I should have sent out for food." He actually looked somewhat embarrassed at his oversight. "I'm sorry. I just have a tendency to get caught up in what I'm doing, and I guess I forgot all about food."

She nodded, understanding the problem. "I think that's part of the reason why Travis left earlier. He and food can't stay apart for very long. He might not show it, but that very mild looking guy gets very grumpy if he and food are separated for more than a few hours." She grinned as she looked at Danny. "I take it that's not your problem."

"When I get caught up in a case, I totally forget about eating, sleeping—you name it," Danny confessed.

Cassandra gave him a once-over. "Well, that explains why you don't seem to have an ounce of fat on you."

"Thanks—I think," Danny said a bit uncertainly.

"Nothing to think about," she told him. "That was a compliment."

"Are California women always this outspoken?" he asked her. It seemed as if from the moment he had met her, the woman had spoken exactly what was on her mind.

"I wouldn't know about California women," she told him. "But we Cavanaugh women are—politely so," she said. "But we've also been known to speak our minds on occasion."

A smile played along his lips. "Yes, I've noticed." He exhaled as he closed down his computer. "Well, Detective Cavanaugh, I think maybe we should call it a night. We've made enough decent headway for one day," he said, nodding at the folders Cassandra had stacked on the desk she was using as well as the folders on his own. "Do you want to grab some takeout or stop at a pizzeria?" he asked, referring to what they had had yesterday.

"That sounds great, but to be very honest, right now I feel as if I'm just too tired to chew," she admitted. She stretched a little because she had gotten so stiff from sitting there and wound up yawning as well. "I think I'm going to call that Uber now," she said, pushing her chair back from the desk and rising to her feet.

"No, you're not," Danny told her.

She blinked. "Excuse me?"

"I said, you're not calling an Uber," he told her. "Not while I'm at your disposal." Danny rose and pushed his chair back under the desk.

"That would be imposing," she protested. Although not too stringently.

"No, that would refer to working as a team," he

said, correcting her. "Team members are there for each other. Or don't you do things like that in California?" he asked.

"We most definitely do, do things like that in California," she told him. She blew out a breath. More than anything, she hated imposing, but she hated arguing about it even more. Besides, she was too tired to be making all that much sense at the moment. "Okay, you can take me to the hotel," she told Danny.

"Oh I can, can I?" he pretended to ask hopefully.

She found herself laughing, and it felt good. "You are crazy. You know that, don't you?" she asked, doubling up her fist and punching him in the arm.

She had a hard punch, he caught himself thinking, massaging his arm. "I'm beginning to realize that," he told her. "Okay, let's go, champ," he told Cassandra, ushering her out of the room.

Danny switched off the light before closing the door.

Chapter 11

It felt as if time had just stood still. Cassandra, her cousin and the New York detectives working on the newly formed task force that revolved around the bodies left behind by the serial killer were all back in the conference room again. They were going through the folders that had been compiled, searching for a common thread.

In truth, two weeks had passed by. And the only common thread that Cassandra and the others were able to find was that the victims they had been able to identify at this point were all males.

Good-looking males by most standards, Cassandra noted.

If this was a small town where a person's idiosyncrasies might stand out, or at least be a thing of pub-

lic knowledge, this tendency for having handsome
men of a certain age just disappear would be much
easier to track down, Cassandra thought.

She could feel a headache beginning to build. She
massaged the bridge of her nose as she reread a para-
graph for what felt like at least the hundredth time.

Closing her eyes, she exhaled impatiently. It was
actually more like the third or fourth time, she admitted silently. But it certainly felt like the hundredth
time. As it was, there were so many small details that
had been compiled, and they had a tendency to swallow and obliterate some of the other facts.

God, her head was killing her, she thought—and
her eyes felt as if they were going to pop out at any
second. She closed them, willing her headache to
go away.

It wasn't listening.

When she opened her eyes again, she found herself looking down at a bottle of aspirin that had been
placed right in front of her. Momentarily bewildered,
Cassandra slowly turned her head to see where the
aspirin had come from.

Danny was standing not that far from her right
side, smiling at her. He gestured toward the half-
filled bottle.

"You look like you could really use a couple of
those," he told her.

Cassandra picked up the bottle and studied it for
a moment. "I could probably use the whole bottle,"
she quipped. "But I wouldn't want to steal your sup-

ply. If this is what you have to deal with on a regular basis, you'll probably wind up needing this a lot more than I do," she told the detective.

"It's not mine," Danny told her, not that it mattered one way or another to his way of thinking. "I got it from the clerk who delivers our mail."

She picked up the half-empty container of pills, looking at it for no apparent reason. This headache was really bad, she thought.

"The mail guy, huh?" she repeated. She thought for a moment, then realized who he had to be referring to. "You mean the guy who pushes that mail cart through here a couple of times a day? The tall guy with the bulging biceps?" she added. She had already decided that when he wasn't here, the guy had to spend the rest of his time in the gym. No one was born with biceps like that.

Danny nodded with a grin. "That would be him," the detective confirmed.

She looked at the small bottle, considering it. She could see the guy bringing mail and packages and even dropping off interoffice memos, but aspirin bottles? That seemed to be over and above the call of duty.

She handed the bottle back to Danny, who wouldn't accept it. "Isn't this rather a strange thing for him to offer you?"

"Take a couple," he urged, then went on to say, "It's all part of Curtis looking out for us," Danny told her.

"Curtis?" she repeated, surprised that the detective knew the mail clerk's name. Danny didn't strike her as the type to make note of something like that.

"Curtis Wayfare," Danny's partner, Lee, filled in. He looked at Danny for confirmation. "I've got to admit that the service has gotten a lot better since Wayfare started working here a couple of years ago. No wrong deliveries, everything delivered on time. The guy comes in early, stays late until the day's job is done. Everyone should take the kind of pride in their work that Wayfare does."

"And providing the aspirin is part of that?" Cassandra asked, having trouble hiding her amusement.

Danny shrugged. "Like I said, the guy watches out for us. The last guy we had used to toss things on our desks, usually the wrong desk," he specified.

"Between you and me," Lee confided, "I think that work—and working out—is all that guy has. He's kind of shy as well."

"What makes you say that?" Travis asked. He had picked up the thread of the conversation as he came over to grab another stack of missing persons folders.

"The guy likes to talk—mainly to my friend Danny here," Lee said, nodding at his partner. "I think if he wasn't so conscientious about doing a good job, he'd shoot the breeze all day with Danny."

Danny waved off the speculation. "I think that's just because my desk is the closest to the exit."

Cassandra supposed that made sense, but she wasn't 100 percent convinced of that, she thought.

The guy gave off a vibe that she couldn't quite put her finger on.

The next minute, she was opening the aspirin bottle and popping two pills.

Mentally crossing her fingers, Cassandra got back to work.

She was so involved in what she was doing, she was oblivious to everything else. The next time that the creaky noise made by the mail cart's wheels penetrated her consciousness, Cassandra looked up, startled. Looking around, she zeroed in on the man's location.

She flashed a smile in the clerk's direction. "Your aspirin did the trick," she informed Wayfare once the man had drawn closer.

Wayfare dropped off a package on a nearby desk. He looked somewhat perplexed by Cassandra's reference. "Excuse me?"

She realized that the man had no idea what she was talking about. "Detective Doyle offered me the bottle of aspirin you gave him," she explained.

For a moment, Cassandra was unable to read the expression that came over the man's features. And then a spasmodic smile lifted the corners of his mouth as the man said, "Glad to hear that it helped. Headaches can totally disorient you and wipe you out."

She could have sworn that she made out what looked to be disappointment pass over the clerk's features. His dark eyes clouded over and his jaw slackened. And then he pulled back his shoulders and told her, "If you'll excuse me, I have to get back to work. I don't want to fall behind." With that, he began to push the cart away from her desk.

Cassandra couldn't help wondering if he was holding on to the sides of the cart in what appeared to be a rather exaggerated motion as he walked by Danny's desk. When the detective didn't look up at him, she thought she heard Wayfare sigh to himself. But then, that could have very well been her imagination.

This case was getting to her, Cassandra told herself.

"Any word from that cousin of yours?" Danny asked right after Wayfare had gone on to another department.

Cassandra laughed as she looked up. "Detective, you're going to have to be a lot more specific than that. I have literally a *ton* of cousins," she said.

He frowned. There was only one of her cousins that mattered in this conversation. "I'm talking about the computer wizard."

Buried the way Cassandra was in the center of all this paperwork, she had all but forgotten the call she had placed to Valri.

A call that hadn't been returned yet.

"Thanks for reminding me," she said as she pulled out her cell phone. She glanced at the screen to see if she had somehow missed a call, but she hadn't.

This wasn't like Valri, she thought as a wave of concern washed over her.

It took Cassandra three tries to get through to her. The call kept getting cut off with a strange busy signal. She had a feeling they had a bad connection.

But finally, her call went through.

"Valri, it's Cass. Are you all right?" she asked the minute she recognized her cousin's voice on the other end.

"Other than drowning in paperwork, yes, I am. Why do you ask?" Valri wanted to know.

"Well, you never returned my call," she told Valri.

"Oh, I thought you were just being nice and giving me some space," her cousin confessed. "Seeing how overwhelmed with paperwork you knew I was," she told Cassandra.

Cassandra sighed. She should have known better than to worry. Her cousin had a way of being able to bounce back no matter what.

"Val, when have I ever been nice?" Cassandra teased.

"Good point," Valri agreed.

Cassandra heard the rustle of paper and assumed that her cousin was retrieving some pages. From the sound of it, Valri went on to draw them over to the phone.

"I didn't find much," Valri confessed.

Cassandra tamped down the disappointment she felt rising within her. Maybe Valri was being modest. "What did you find?" she pressed. "Do you have any indication of who Nathan's friends were, who he hung around with, anything at all like that?"

"Well, what I have here is that when our wayward cousin wasn't hanging out with a whole bevy of sexy women, he liked to go to the gym to build up his body so he could continue attracting those women."

"And that's it?" she asked, unable to keep the disappointment out of her voice. "No names? Did he use a particular trainer or teacher?" she wanted to know. "C'mon, Val," she begged, "I need a name. Something to start me out."

"The only name I could find was this young guy, Carl Wilson," she told Cassandra. "He attended the gym at the same time that our cousin did. Nathan disappeared, and from what I can tell, so did this Carl guy. I know this doesn't exactly help," she told Cassandra.

"Well, we now know something more than we did before," she told Valri. As she spoke, a thought came to her. It wasn't anything concrete, but maybe it would lead to something. "They both belonged to that gym, didn't they?"

"Yes. I just said that," Valri reminded her.

"Can you get me the name of that gym and see if they had membership cards with their photos on them on file? I think that was about the time when clubs and corporations began to keep records like that."

"It's definitely worth a try," Valri agreed, then

said, "That is, if the gym didn't close down or get replaced by some sort of other business."

"It might have just changed hands or even names," Cassandra said, reviewing the possibilities. "It's been known to happen."

"Okay, I'll check it out and get back to you," the woman everyone at the precinct thought of as "the computer wizard" told her.

"Great, but this time, do me a favor and try not to bury this," Cassandra requested.

By her tone of voice, it was obvious that Valri thought she had this coming to her. "I am really sorry about that," her cousin said. "It won't happen again, Cass, I promise."

"I guess you are human after all," Cassandra told her with a soft laugh.

"All too human," Valri admitted.

After another moment, the call between them terminated.

Tucking the phone away, she saw Danny and her cousin Travis looking at her. Danny spoke up first.

"Well?" the detective asked. "What did she have to say?"

"Valri promised to get back to me. She said she forgot to call us back because she just got buried in work and she didn't realize that we were in a hurry," Cassandra explained.

"How could she not realize that?" Travis wanted to know.

"The point is that she didn't. But we're not dead in the water yet," Cassandra told the two men.

"I'll believe it when I see it," Danny told her.

"Wow, talk about being a skeptic," Cassandra marveled, shaking her head.

"Hey, I'm a detective," he reminded her. "I'm supposed to be skeptical, not gullible."

"Nobody said anything about being gullible," she reminded him. "Valri is going to get back to me about the trainer or guy who worked out or trained with Nathan. Who knows, if we can locate the guy, maybe he can point us in the right direction. You just never know when one of these details could amount to something," she told the other men.

Danny looked far from impressed about the lack of information, but he had to agree that Cassandra might be onto something. In any event, it was a good place to begin the following morning.

"You're right," he said to Cassandra, reluctantly agreeing. "Okay, why don't we order in and get some dinner, then call it a night?" he suggested. "Requests?" he asked, looking around the room.

Cassandra held up her hand. "I want to know who's paying for all this," she asked. "We've been eating pizza, Chinese takeout and the like, and neither Travis nor I have contributed toward any of the cost. Are you going to hit us with a tab at the end?" she wanted to know.

"Don't worry about it. The NYPD's pockets are deep enough to cover a few sandwiches and takeout orders. Besides, it's the chief's way of saying thanks for the help."

Cassandra backed off a little. "Well, I've learned never to argue with authority figures," she told the New York detective flippantly.

Danny met her comment with a dismissive laugh. "Yeah, right. Like I believe that."

"You should," Cassandra told him. "Because I'm very serious. I don't argue with authority figures—I might, however, attempt to chip away at their armor with very small swings, but nothing that would crack their exterior," she told the detective. "At least, not all at once."

"Don't worry about it. Now, pizza or Chinese food?" Danny wanted to know, referring to the two items she had asked for during the week.

Cassandra answered without thinking. "Pizza," she told him. "It tastes good hot or cold." She thought for a moment. "You know, we need to find a way to solve these cold cases soon. Otherwise, I am going to wind up gaining an *awful* lot of weight," she confessed. Her mouth curved. "In case you haven't noticed, I just can't say no to pizza."

Danny looked at her, feigning an innocent expression. "Nope, did not notice that," he told her.

Travis, who had said very little up to this point, content with just observing his cousin, couldn't get over the difference he'd noticed in Cassandra. Usually, she was all business, applying herself to the evidence in front of her and exclusively attempting to solve the giant, disjointed jigsaw puzzle and nothing more.

Now, if he read the look in his cousin's eyes correctly, she was also involved in something beyond just solving the case.

The case, of course, was *always* exceedingly important to her; it always had been since she had begun working on the police department. However, he saw that there was room for something else, something more. She seemed to be very taken with the detective that she had—just a couple of weeks ago—locked horns with when she first arrived in New York.

Now, apparently, she had backed off.

It was going to be interesting to see where this was going to lead, he thought. But obviously not tonight.

Stifling a yawn, Travis hoped the food would get here soon.

Chapter 12

"You know, I get this feeling that we're missing something. Like we're circling around the solution, and it's right there in front of us, but we're just not able to put our finger on it," Cassandra told Danny. She was clearly frustrated.

Dinner had come and gone. When they were finished eating, Danny had brought the two Cavanaughs to their hotel.

Exhausted, Travis went to his room immediately, but when it came time for Cassandra to go in to hers, she and Danny both found that they weren't ready to call it a night yet, despite the late hour. They caught themselves talking about and sharing theories that struck them about the elusive killer who had robbed so many young men of their lives.

They were still talking when they finally got out of Danny's vehicle. Neither one hardly remembered taking the elevator to her room.

Cassandra stood by the door and turned toward the detective. "Would you like to come in?" she asked him. "They put in one of those cute little coffeemakers in my room. We can have coffee and brainstorm a little more."

The New York detective glanced at his watch. "Coffee?" he questioned. "At this hour? Don't you want to get *any* sleep?"

Cassandra was caught off guard by the detective's question. "Oh, coffee won't keep me up," she told him. Using her keycard, she opened the door and let the detective into the room.

Danny peered over the threshold, debating coming in. "Really?" He was looking at her skeptically.

"Really," Cassandra answered. "You could inject a mug of coffee into my bloodstream, and it really wouldn't have any effect on me." She saw the doubtful look on his face intensify and assured him, "I've been like this ever since I was a kid. But if you're too tired…" she said, her voice trailing off.

Danny gestured toward the opened hotel door. "Lead the way. I think I can keep my eyes opened long enough to learn something new," he told Cassandra.

That was when she had said to him that she felt as if they were overlooking something, missing something that was right in front of them. She went on to admit that she had nothing concrete to point to, that it was more of a feeling she had. A *gut* feeling, something some of her uncles and cousins were partial to pointing to.

Some of them, she went on to tell the detective, even swore by that feeling. She knew it sounded fanciful, but at the same time, she would have bet anything that she was experiencing the very same feeling that her cousins and uncles had right now.

The feeling just seemed to run too deep, too strong, to be fanciful.

"Okay, what do you think we're missing?" Danny asked her patiently.

Cassandra laughed softly. "If I knew that," she said with emphasis, "the pieces would fall into place instead of just floating around aimlessly in my head." With that, she tossed a rather thick folder onto her bed.

He looked at her in surprise. "You brought the folders to the hotel with you?"

That didn't seem like something that she would be inclined to do, not without asking permission and signing the folders out, at any rate.

"No, these aren't the actual folders. I made copies and brought those with me," she told the detective. Cassandra smiled at him. "I know better than to take the actual folders out of the precinct." Her eyes met his. "I wouldn't want to bring down the wrath of the New York Police Department on my head."

"No wrath," Danny told her with a straight face.

And then he grinned. "We would just hang you out to dry, that's all."

The corners of her mouth curved in amusement. "Well, no need for that," she told the detective. "We might be a little unorthodox where I come from, but we do make a point of following all the rules. Or at least the ones that make sense."

He nodded. "Never meant to suggest that you didn't."

Cassandra smiled at the man in her hotel room. "I appreciate that," she told him. "Would you like that coffee now?" she offered, then explained the reason for her question. "Your eyes look like they're drooping," she told him. "You're either tired, or I'm boring you."

"Absolutely not," he told her with feeling.

If anything, Danny admitted to himself, he was finding her increasingly stimulating. He had, of course, already noticed that she was a very beautiful woman. But beauty all by itself had never really moved the detective beyond a certain point.

There was something about the look in Cassandra's incredibly green eyes, something about the way her mouth curved at the corners when she was beyond amused, that he found almost hypnotically inviting.

It spoke to him, moved him.

At first, he tried very hard not to dwell on his reaction to her, but as time went by, he was finding that response far more difficult to bury than he had first thought.

She smiled at Danny's almost enthusiastic response to her question. "So, tell me out of sheer curiosity, do you have any theories about who this serial killer might be? Do you think he's someone who just randomly stumbled across these people, and for whatever reason, they brought out his killing instincts? Or was this something that the killer found himself planning because of his response to that person? Something that he felt compelled to carry out?" Asking the question, she studied his reaction to it.

She might have been studying him, but Danny caught himself studying her as well. He was caught up in watching the way her lips moved as she formed her questions.

With effort, Danny forced himself to look away from Cassandra. He couldn't allow himself to get carried away by this woman. There were far more important things at stake here than watching the way her lips moved as she worded her questions.

Danny thought for a moment, considering what she had just asked him. "I guess that's where the investigation comes in."

She thought of her own reaction to the situation. "You've got to have a gut feeling about it," she told him with simple solemnity.

"Maybe later," he responded. And then, to lighten the conversation, he just changed its direction. "Did you always want to be a cop?" he asked the attractive woman.

His question, without any preamble, caught her up short. In order to give the detective an honest response, she had to think about it.

When she finally did come up with an answer, it wasn't one that he was expecting.

"James Bond was my hero," she admitted.

His brow furrowed. That didn't make any sense to him. "But he was a guy," Danny said. "Fictional," he said, tagging that on, "but very much a guy."

"More important than that," Cassandra told the detective, "he was someone who righted wrongs, and I have to admit, that aspect always *really* appealed to me."

Danny laughed under his breath as he shook his head. "You are one very strange lady, Cassandra Cavanaugh."

The grin she flashed reached her eyes. "Not sure if you mean it this way, but I'm going to take what you just said as a compliment."

He pretended to assume a serious expression. "I suppose you can, in a way. You certainly are unique, I'll give you that," the detective told her. "So, I suppose my answer to your question is a very roundabout yes," Danny concluded.

"I suppose so," she agreed, nodding her head. "But then, I never saw any sort of other alternative," she told him, referring to her choice of heroes. "All my heroes were police detectives."

Danny thought of the era she was referring to. "Men," Danny said. Back then most of the detectives were men, he recalled.

"Except for the policewoman who was Uncle Brian's partner," she said. "The woman who he eventually went on to marry," Cassandra told him, then, seeing the confusion in Danny's eyes, she said, "It's complicated."

Danny laughed dryly. "I don't think that there's anything straightforward about your family," the detective told her. "At first encounter, they seem to be straightforward enough, completely down-to-earth and all that. But then, after listening to the details for a while, you realize that there is really *nothing* straightforward about any of your family members," he told her.

She grinned, ready to contradict him. "Yes, there is. You're just not accustomed to people like us," she told him matter-of-factly.

Her grin grew as a shine entered her eyes. "We're just different."

Danny shook his head and shrugged. That wouldn't have been his word for it, he thought, but she seemed to be rather comfortable with it.

"I suppose that's one way to describe it," Danny told her. "But then," he said, as another thought occurred to him, "maybe I'm just being jealous."

He had managed to surprise her again, she thought.

Cassandra blinked after she all but drained the remainder of her coffee. "Excuse me?"

"Maybe I'm admitting too much," he told her uncomfortably.

Oh, no, she wasn't about to have him back away now. "Sorry, you can't just stop now. *Why* are you jealous?" Cassandra wanted to know.

He had started this, but it was too late to back away now. Danny took a breath before launching into his explanation. "You have this really big family…" he began.

"There's no denying that," she said, the corners of her mouth curving. She had gathered that Danny's family was next to nonexistent.

He moved over to the window. It looked down at Sixth Avenue, six stories below. Danny had his hands wrapped around what was left of the cup of hot inkyblack coffee. He could feel the warmth sinking deep into his soul.

"After my aunt just disappeared," he remembered, "there was just my mother and me. And then she came down with leukemia."

His voice grew still. "I just couldn't seem to spend enough time with her—at least not enough time to make a difference." He worked at keeping the sadness out of his voice. "Certainly not enough time to gather up into some imaginary mental sack that I could hold on to and occasionally peek into whenever I felt the overwhelming need to remember her."

He turned from the window and saw the startled way Cassandra was looking at him as she listened to what he was telling her.

Danny flushed. "Sorry, I think I'm just getting punchy," he said. He set his cup on the counter next to the coffeemaker. "I'd better get going."

He still looked rather bleary-eyed to her.

"I don't think you're in any shape to drive, Detective," she told him.

"Well, clicking my heels together and saying, 'There's no place like home,' isn't an option at the moment, so I guess that just leaves driving," he told her.

"No, there is another option on the table," Cassandra told him.

Okay, she had made him curious. "And that is?" Danny asked, at a loss as to what she was referring to. He really doubted that she was suggesting what he thought she was suggesting. She struck him as too straitlaced for that.

"You can sack out on the sofa," she told him matter-of-factly. "Or, if for some reason that isn't comfortable for your back, you can take the bed, and I can take the sofa," she told him.

He wasn't expecting that. Yes, he was tired, but spending the night in the same room with her struck him as far too tempting, exhausted though he was.

Danny shook his head. "That's okay," he began, only to have Cassandra cut him short.

"No, it's not okay," she informed him, her voice taking on an authoritative tone. "I am not having you fall asleep behind the wheel of your car."

"I just finished the coffee you felt you had to

Get up to 4
FREE FABULOUS BOOKS
You Love!

To thank you for being a loyal reader we'd like to send you up to 4 FREE BOOKS, absolutely free when you try the Harlequin Reader Service.

Just write "YES" on the Loyal Reader Voucher and we'll send you 2 free books from each series you choose and Free Mystery Gifts, altogether worth over $20.

Try **Harlequin® Romantic Suspense** books featuring heart-racing page-turners with unexpected plot twists and irresistible chemistry that will keep you guessing to the very end.

Try **Harlequin Intrigue® Larger-Print** books featuring action-packed stories that will keep you on the edge of your seat. Solve the crime and deliver justice at all costs.

Or **TRY BOTH and get 2 books from each series!**

Your free books are completely free, even the shipping! If you continue with your subscription, you can look forward to curated monthly shipments of brand-new books from your selected series, always at a discount off the cover price! Plus you can cancel any time.

So don't miss out, return your Loyal Readers Voucher today to get your Free books.

Pam Powers

LOYAL READER
FREE BOOKS VOUCHER

YES! I Love Reading, please send me up to 4 FREE BOOKS and Free Mystery Gifts from the series I select.

Just write in "YES" on the dotted line below then return this card today and we'll send your free books & gifts asap!

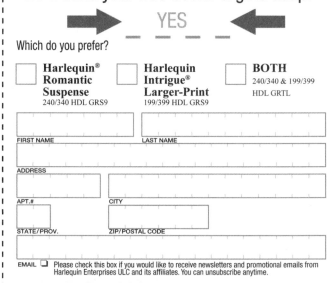

YES

Which do you prefer?

☐ **Harlequin® Romantic Suspense**
240/340 HDL GRS9

☐ **Harlequin Intrigue® Larger-Print**
199/399 HDL GRS9

☐ **BOTH**
240/340 & 199/399
HDL GRTL

FIRST NAME	**LAST NAME**
ADDRESS	
APT.#	**CITY**
STATE/PROV.	**ZIP/POSTAL CODE**

EMAIL ☐ Please check this box if you would like to receive newsletters and promotional emails from Harlequin Enterprises ULC and its affiliates. You can unsubscribe anytime.

HI/HRS-622-LR_LRV22

offer me." Danny nodded at the large mug he had put down. It was now all but empty.

"I can see that," she told him. "And for some reason, it didn't seem to kick in the way you thought it would," Cassandra said. "Now, you either get a room here for the night, or you take me up on my offer and my sofa and spend the night here."

She could see that Danny was about to argue with her, and she cut him off before he could get started. "I refuse to be responsible for them finding your body embedded in what's left of your vehicle. Now stop arguing with me," she ordered. "You know I'm right."

Danny sighed. "Yeah, I do," he said. "But even if I didn't, I've got the feeling that you wouldn't let me win this argument."

"And that's what makes you such a good detective," she told him with a wide smile.

He looked down at what he was wearing. "I don't have a change of clothing with me," he said.

"No go-bag in your trunk?" Cassandra asked him.

"No what?" he questioned.

"Never mind," she assured him, waving away the term she had used. "No one is going to grade you on the fact that you are wearing the same thing two days in a row. The only thing that counts is finding this serial killer," Cassandra told him, then amended her statement. "Or at least getting close to solving this thing. I assure you that the people who work with you will take more note of the news headline in tomorrow morning's paper about the cold case detective who was found plastered against the inside of the windshield within his extremely mangled vehicle."

Tired, he still had to laugh as he shook his head. "You have a really colorful imagination."

"No, what I have is the memory of a friend who insisted on driving home when he shouldn't have—and the guilt of my not putting my foot down and insisting that he not drive in his present, drowsy condition. Now stop arguing with me," she said. "I need my sleep."

And with that, she gathered up a pillow and blanket, spread out the latter on the sofa, and then, satisfied that she had done her best, she turned around and laid down, fully dressed, on her bed.

She was asleep within ten minutes.

Chapter 13

He frowned to himself as he stared up at the building.

He knew for a fact that Detective Doyle had ridden up with that two-bit California detective, and Doyle hadn't come down yet.

That meant that he was still up there with her.

His frown grew deeper. He had taken an instant dislike to her the moment he had seen her walking in through the door of the precinct. She had that know-it-all look about her, the kind he had seen on so many women's faces when he was growing up, he thought, his face growing darker.

The kind that made him angry.

Very angry.

As he felt himself growing progressively angrier, he decided to ride up to the visiting detective's floor.

Every time he'd heard the elevator bell go off, he could feel himself growing increasingly more up-tight. It took effort to control his breathing.

Getting off on the sixth floor, he was carefully watching the signals that were coming from the state-of-the-art tracking device that he had managed to slip into Doyle's pocket earlier today. He had done it while he was distributing the mail.

A pleased smile lifted the corners of his full mouth. At the same time, he could feel himself getting angrier and angrier because that tramp was still in there with Doyle. Having her here could spoil everything.

It could lay waste to all his carefully laid plans, causing them to crumble.

Moving quietly, he made his way past the hotel door. Because of the late hour and the fact that it was the middle of the week, there was no noise coming from the room.

Any of the rooms, actually.

He stared at the door as if he could actually see through it and into the room. Detective Doyle and that worthless two-bit who had clamped onto him had worn themselves out. He could just *sense* it.

As he thought about the circumstances behind the silence, his face grew progressively redder and redder as his eyes all but bored holes into the door.

At that moment, he heard someone coming down the hallway. Instantly alert, he moved in the opposite direction, making his way toward the stairs.

He wasn't about to take the elevator and risk running into anyone. The chances were incredibly slim, but he knew that he *could* wind up running into someone from the precinct.

He supposed he could explain it away by saying that he was visiting someone here, but then he might be asked to identify that person, which meant that he might have to kill the person who was questioning him, because he didn't have a ready name to offer up.

He could feel his adrenaline rising as he made his way quickly down the stairs. Reaching the ground floor took no time at all. Neither did taking a side door.

The woman would pay, he promised himself, his fists clenched at his sides. Maybe not right now. But soon.

Very soon.

Envisioning the scene, he took comfort in that.

Stifling a yawn, Cassandra slipped out of bed, went into the bathroom and threw some cold water on her face.

It was time to start getting ready, she told herself. She and Danny had spent too much time together, talking as well as enjoying each other's company.

A couple of times she had even thought that the distance between them was going to melt away and that their lips would wind up making contact. Deep contact.

That was just wishful thinking, Cassandra told herself. She had no idea why her mind had even gone that route. It wasn't as if anything even remotely romantic had passed between them except for that one fleeting kiss she had delivered that first evening.

Last night she had just gotten punchy, she told herself.

Splashing water on her face to wake up, she came out of the bathroom and wound up swallowing the scream that had instantly sprang to her lips. She had walked out of the bathroom and directly into Danny.

Swaying, she appeared so startled, Danny grabbed hold of her shoulders to keep her from toppling over. Otherwise, he was fairly certain that she would have wound up unintentionally hitting the floor.

"Hey, steady there," Danny said, just as startled as she was. "I can't be that scary first thing in the morning—can I?" It sounded like a genuine question.

She could feel her heart pounding against her ribcage. It took her a moment to get her pulse to settle down.

"You're not," she told him. "It's just that when I left you, you were completely dead asleep, and I walked back in less than ten minutes later, you're wide awake and look as if you're ready to leap into the fray."

His forehead furrowed. Maybe he was still dreaming. The woman wasn't making any sense. "You want to run that by me again?"

But Cassandra shook her head, waving away her words. "Never mind," she told the detective, then suggested, "Why don't you take a shower and we'll get going?"

"Are you telling me that I smell?" he asked her, pretending to be offended while keeping an innocent expression.

"What? No," she said in vehement denial. "I just thought that since you slept in the clothes you had on yesterday, you might want to refresh yourself a little. But you don't have to," she told him quickly.

His eyes swept over her. For a moment, he could almost *see* her taking a shower. "How about you?" he asked. "Or did you already take a shower?"

"Actually, no," she said. "I wanted to make sure that you made use of the bathroom if you had to before I got into the shower."

"That sounds as if you had a couple of bad experiences," he said, amusement playing on his lips.

"I did. As a kid," Cassandra specified, "but it did make me very leery. Long story short," she told him, "the bathroom is all yours if you need it."

Danny nodded. "Be out in a few minutes," he promised.

And he was, she noted, amazing her, to say the least. Barely seven minutes had gone by, and Danny emerged out of the hotel bathroom, toweling his hair dry.

Cassandra looked at the man in unabashed surprise.

Her brothers would have definitely taken longer, especially Campbell. "That *was* fast," she told him.

He laughed at her comment. At this point, Danny sincerely doubted if he knew *how* to take a slow shower. He had gotten into the habit of being speedy early on out of sheer necessity.

"When I was a kid, between my mother and my aunt and me, taking showers—quick ones, mind you—the hot water ran out really fast," he said. "I got really good at taking what I felt, at the time, were the world's fastest showers.

"When our landlord got around to replacing our ancient water heater and we actually had hot water for longer than three minutes at a time, I was already trained to take really fast showers."

The smile that lifted his lips was a fond one as he thought back to those days. "Anyway, it was a good habit to get into, I guess. It keeps my water bill down and within reason."

Cassandra laughed. "I wish you had been around to talk to my brothers back in the day," she told him. Glancing at her watch, she was ready to go. "What do you say we grab some take-out breakfast on the way to the precinct?"

Danny nodded. "Sounds good to me. Why don't you go and wake up your cousin?" he suggested, nodding toward the outer door.

His words were met with a wide smile from Cassandra. "You're beginning to get to know how we Cavanaughs operate," she told him.

"We New York cops are not known to be slow on the uptake," he told her matter-of-factly.

"Yes," Cassandra answered, her eyes slowly washing over the detective. She kept finding herself responding to the man. "I guess I am definitely beginning to see that."

Maybe, Cassandra silently lectured herself, she needed not to look at him so much. There was something about Danny Doyle that really drew her in, and the more she looked at him, the more drawn to him she was.

That wasn't usually the case for her when it came to men. The more she was around them, the less attracted to them she became. She found things that wound up turning her off.

But this was different, she realized. The more time she spent around Danny, the more she found herself liking him. Trying to understand why only made things more complicated, she thought.

The case, damn it, Cavanaugh. Focus on the case, not the man's compelling green eyes or his really muscular biceps, Cassandra said, scolding herself.

Taking their winter coats with them, they went out into the hall and stopped two doors down. Cassandra knocked on Travis's door.

There was no answer. She tried again.

It took three knocks, each progressively louder, on her cousin's door before it finally opened.

Her cousin, looking as if he were dead asleep on his feet, mumbled a greeting at them as he took a step back, opening the door wider.

"Is it morning already?" Travis asked in a raspy voice.

"Yes, and you'd know that if you looked out your

window," Cassandra told him, pointing toward the daylight that was just beginning to stream in.

Travis stifled a yawn. "I'm still on California time," her cousin told her. "Besides, windows are for watching pretty girls walk by, not for measuring the time," Travis said, stifling yet another yawn as he attempted to rub the sleep out of his eyes.

It didn't work. He still appeared to be very bleary-eyed.

"That would be a little difficult on the sixth floor," Danny said.

"I didn't say it was easy," Travis mumbled. He felt as if there was wad of cotton in his mouth. He rubbed his eyes again. "Just give me a couple of minutes to get dressed," he told Cassandra and the detective.

"Travis, you *are* dressed," Cassandra said.

Travis looked down at what he was wearing, more surprised than they were to find himself wearing clothes.

"Oh yeah, I am." Travis responded. "I can't remember if I tumbled into bed fully dressed or got dressed in my sleep this morning." He stifled yet another yawn. "I think I got dressed this morning," he said more to himself than to Cassandra and Doyle.

Cassandra leaned into Travis, taking in a long breath as she gave her cousin the once-over. "That would be my guess," she told him. "Now, are you ready to go, or should Doyle and I here each grab one arm and just drag you out into the hallway?"

Travis drew himself up indignantly. "I can walk on my own power," he told his cousin.

"Yes, Virginia, there is a Santa Claus," Cassandra declared with a laugh. She led the way back out again.

The trio took the elevator down to the first floor and then made their way out of the hotel.

"Do you remember where you left the car?" she asked Doyle.

"Always," he told her. "My basic survival depends on it."

He led the way back to where he had left his vehicle in the parking structure and drove it out onto the street.

Cassandra didn't say anything to either of the two men, but throughout it all, as well as the trip back to the precinct, it felt as if they had never left. And she just couldn't seem to shake the feeling that they or, at the very least, she was being watched.

Which just didn't seem possible, she told herself.

I really am getting paranoid, Cassandra thought.

Even so, she could have sworn that she felt eyes all but drilling into the back of her head. Why? She hadn't felt that there was someone watching her yesterday morning. No, this feeling was definitely new, she thought.

"Something wrong?" Danny asked as he slowed down at a light and waited for it to turn green again. Glancing at her, he had noted the look on her face.

"You mean other than a madman running around killing people?" she asked him.

"Yes, other than that," he answered.

She debated telling the detective about the uneasy feeling she'd been struggling with, but she was fairly convinced that he would tell her that she was being paranoid, or something along those lines. Cassandra didn't want him thinking less of her.

"No, I'm just thinking," she told him.

"About?" Danny prodded. She couldn't tell if he was genuinely interested or just giving her a hard time.

She shrugged, avoiding his eyes. "Just stuff."

"Like?" he wanted to know. Then prodded when she didn't answer. "C'mon, out with it. What's on your mind? What's bugging you?" Danny asked point-blank.

She sighed. The man wasn't going to let up until she gave him something. And then she would have something new to regret, she thought.

"All right, if you must know," she told him in slow, measured words, "I can't shake the feeling that—" And then, at the last minute, she changed her mind, dismissing her feelings. "Never mind."

But Danny refused to back off. "No, you started this," he told her. "So, out with it. What's bother you?"

She closed her eyes and sighed, then, opening them again, she said, "All right, you asked for this," she told him impatiently. "I can't shake the feeling that there's someone watching me. There," she declared. "Are you satisfied? Go ahead. Say it."

He was driving again, so it took a moment before he could spare Cassandra a fleeting glance. "Say what?"

"That I'm getting paranoid or letting the serial killer get to me or something equally as critical of my thought process."

A serious expression slipped over the New York detective's face. "I can't, because I'm don't think that you're wrong," Danny told her in a quiet voice.

It was hard for Cassandra to keep her mouth from dropping open. She glanced over her shoulder to exchange looks with her cousin. For the life of her, she couldn't figure out if Danny was putting her on—or not.

But it didn't sound like it.

Chapter 14

"Can you repeat that?" Cassandra said, looking at the detective.

She wasn't sure if Danny was actually being serious—or if he was just having fun at her expense. She would have liked to think that he was being serious, but in all honesty, she still didn't know him well enough to make that judgment call.

"You heard me the first time, Detective," Danny told her, certain that she had. And then, just to be sure, he repeated it. "I don't think that you're wrong."

He sighed, debating the significance of the admission he had just made. He might as well get all of it out, he thought. "Something keeps sticking in my craw," he admitted. "I would have said that you were being paranoid—that *I* was being paranoid," he underscored. "Except that…" His voice trailed off, and then he almost wound up saying the words to himself rather than to her. "Except that," he repeated, "I can't seem to shake the feeling that there is someone watching us.

"With a case of this magnitude, I guess that's not unusual," he went on to say softly, as if some invisible voice had whispered those words into his ear.

He had a point, Cassandra thought, focusing on what he had just said. But still, she couldn't separate herself from the feeling that there was something more to this whole set up, something they were all somehow missing.

She sighed. "We *really* need to get to the bottom of this," Cassandra said to the two detectives in the car as she turned in her seat to look first at her cousin, then back at Danny. "First thing I'm going to do once we reach the office is to call Valri to see if she's made any headway compiling that list of people that the victims were in contact with just before they summarily went missing."

She pressed her lips together, thinking. "Maybe that'll point us in the right direction so we can actually begin solving this thing and finally find that serial killer."

"Maybe you should make that the second thing," Travis said. "Don't forget, our computer wizard is three hours behind us timewise. She probably feels exactly the way that I do right now—punchy and sleepy." Cassandra's cousin punctuated his statement with a huge yawn.

"Punchy," Cassandra repeated. "Is that by any chance the name of Snow White's eighth dwarf?" she asked, humor curving the corners of her mouth. "In any case," she told her cousin more seriously, "Valri's not like the rest of us. You know that," she insisted. "The woman runs on batteries and can multitask better than all the rest of us put together," she said, reminding Travis. "At any rate, the sooner we get our hands on this list once she puts it together, the sooner we can begin finding and investigating these people. And that, in turn, gets us closer to finding this fiend and putting him away. Permanently," Cassandra said, stressing that last word with feeling.

"You know, it might not be a man," Travis said.

He was wrong there, she thought. This could not have been the work of a woman for one good reason.

Cassandra smiled to herself. "If it's a woman doing this, then it's a woman who is capable of bench-pressing at least two hundred pounds, if not more. These are not skinny, underweight little men who are being hauled out and done away with," she said. "From the photographs I saw in the files, every one of the victims were all full-sized men. Dragging them out of sight, picking their bodies apart and then burying them—most likely quickly—required strength," she told her cousin. "A lot of it."

Listening to the conversation, Danny finally pulled his vehicle into the parking structure beneath the precinct. He parked it in his customary spot, pulled up the handbrake and then turned off the engine.

Staying in his seat, the detective turned around to glance back at Travis.

"This is the one time that I'm throwing my vote in with your cousin," he told Travis. Pausing, he cleared his throat, then continued. "Meanwhile, we track down any leads, however slim, however minor," he informed the detectives from California. "There has to be something that we're missing, something that will get us closer to an answer."

He saw Cassandra smiling at him as she got out of his car. That had to mean something.

"What?" Danny prodded, even as he caught himself thinking that maybe he really didn't want to know what was on her mind.

"Nothing," she denied, then went on to tell him, "You know, that's actually a very positive attitude." Her smile deepened. "I'm just surprised—and pleased—to hear those words coming out of your mouth, Detective."

She paused for a moment. There was a sparkle entering her eyes as she looked at him. "It looks like maybe I'm rubbing off on you," Cassandra told him.

Danny looked at her as they walked through the precinct's front doors and made their way to the elevator. The New York detective caught himself thinking that he would have welcomed having the woman actually rubbing off on him.

Or just simply rubbing, Danny mused for a moment.

The next moment, he managed to rouse himself again and focus on something more serious.

The New York detective cleared his throat.

He would have probably found himself getting slapped for the direction his mind was taking.

He attempted to berate himself but just couldn't get his mind to go that route. Instead, he couldn't stop smiling as he thought about the woman who had been assigned to his division.

This was not the proper attitude for an investigator of his caliber to assume, he told himself again, doing his best to pull back.

Danny could see Cassandra looking at him. Her expression was rather bemused. For a fleeting second, the detective thought that with his luck, the woman was probably a mind reader.

Drawing himself together, Danny quickly took refuge in the comment Cassandra had just made about rubbing off on him. "I guess maybe you are at that," he said, then commented, "Lucky me."

"Now that just sounds like sarcasm," Cassandra told the detective.

His mouth quirked just a little as his eyes washed over her almost in slow motion. "Well, you're a detective," he reminded Cassandra. "I'm guessing that you have the tools to figure that out."

He had just sent a definite warm shiver down her spine with that look of his, she realized. "I'll get back to you on that," she heard herself responding, uttering the words almost in slow motion. She cleared her head and went on to say, "Right now, I want to see if Valri came through with something."

With that, she all but marched into the office.

"Let me know if she has anything worthwhile to tell us," Travis requested, calling after his cousin.

"Will do," Cassandra promised, tossing the words over her shoulder.

At that point, she realized that she was not going to the conference room alone. She found that she was being shadowed by Danny.

She glanced at him just as she crossed the threshold. "Is there something you forgot to tell me?" Cassandra asked him.

Danny shook his head. "Nope."

"Then we just happen to be heading in the same direction at the same time?" she asked Danny skeptically.

Danny inclined his head. "Sure looks that way." And then he grew more serious. "Look, I want to know what you know as soon as you know it. Don't forget," the detective reminded her, "this was my case before you ever stepped one foot onto the scene."

Well, if he wanted to play it that way, she thought, she had something to counter him with. "Yes, but he was my cousin before he ever disappeared in your city."

Though she didn't have any knowledge of him. It was like saying she was distantly related to Anne Boleyn. Sure, she could claim a personal need for information, but the case would officially belong to the authorities.

"Tell you what," Danny proposed. "Let's stop playing tug-of-war and just see what this brilliant cousin of yours can tell us about our serial killer."

She inclined her head. "Well, I certainly can't argue with your wording."

Walking into the conference room, she noticed that one of the members of Danny's team was already in the room, going over one of the files, most likely for the umpteenth time if one went by the papers that were all spread out on the man's side of the table.

Danny gave the burly man, Murphy, a dismissive look. "We need the room for a few minutes, Murphy," he told the sergeant.

The man rose from the table. "I think I'll go get some coffee," Murphy told them. "Can I bring back one for either of you?"

Danny reacted with total disbelief. "You've got to be kidding. I wouldn't drink that stuff if I was dying of thirst."

"That was a little drastic, don't you think?" Cassandra asked as the other man left the room.

Danny looked at her knowingly. "You've never tasted the coffee here at the precinct, have you?" It really wasn't a question.

"No," Cassandra agreed, "I haven't."

"Let's just say that I just saved your life," the New York detective told her. There was a laugh in his voice.

The man was steadily growing more animated, Cassandra thought, and that, in her mind, was a good thing. She could definitely deal with animated. *Animated* made the man more human in her book, and more human was always a good thing.

You need to stop focusing on the man and focus on the bigger picture, she told herself sternly. Heaven knew Detective Doyle was already stirring her in ways that she felt were not appropriate on the job— or off the job, for that matter, in her case.

She didn't have any time for all those stirrings that she had heard her friends talk about. At least no time while she was working, she thought—which seemed to be all the time.

And yet, here she was, reacting to being around the man. Reacting to the sound of his voice. Reacting even to the thought of their being together, and not just as a working couple.

Knock it off, Cavanaugh. You have a job to do. Just do it, she ordered herself.

Cassandra became aware that the detective was watching her. Blowing out a breath, she forced herself not to focus on the fact that his eyes were on her.

Picking up her cell phone, Cassandra called the number that she had used so often that it was all but permanently burned into her brain.

The phone rang a total of six times as she waited for Valri to pick up. She thought it was going to ring again. But then she heard a voice on the other end responding.

"Cavanaugh," Valri announced in a very clipped tone of voice.

Cassandra guessed that meant the computer wizard was already swamped at this early hour. Well, she knew that couldn't be helped as she drew back her shoulders.

"Hi, Valri. I'll make this fast," she promised the computer wizard.

"My mistake, I thought this was Cassie," she heard Valri saying to her.

"You know it's me, Valri. I was just trying to be thoughtful," Cassie told the computer wizard in all sincerity.

"Hence my confusion," Valri told her with a laugh. "Is this a little preamble before you tell me that you unearthed something good in your search, or are you trying to entertain me before you pull the rug out from under me and tell me you have nothing to give me that would count as helpful?"

"Which would you like to hear, Cass?" Valri asked.

Cassandra instantly read between the lines and had her answer. "Okay, you have something," she declared happily.

Valri hedged her response. She never liked bragging. "Nothing great, but better than nothing."

She had forgotten that Valri never built things up and definitely did not like tooting her own horn. Out of all of them, Cassandra recalled, Valri was considered to be the most conservative one.

"I'm listening," Cassandra said quietly, waiting.

"Okay, I'm going to text you a couple of pictures."

Cassandra looked down at her phone screen. The images were not all that clear. "Who am I looking at?"

"Guys who were last seen in the company of some of the men who went missing shortly thereafter," Valri told her.

Cassandra continued to stare at the two photographs on her phone. "Valri, is it my imagination, or..."

She heard her cousin laugh. "So, you see it too I take it?"

Danny couldn't pretend not to be listening to this conversation any longer. He looked over Cassandra's shoulder at the photographs that had been sent to her phone. "What is it that you're looking at?" he asked.

The question was no sooner out of his mouth than he realized what the two women who were talking had meant.

He saw it as well.

There was a very strong similarity between the two people in the two photos that had just been sent.

Cassandra raised her eyes to Danny's face. "They could be one and the same person," she said.

"Or they could just be related," Danny said. "Working this job, I've met a lot of brothers who looked as if they were the same person," he told her.

Cassandra got back to asking her cousin questions. "Do you have names for these guys, Valri?"

"Do I have the names?" Valri repeated incredulously. "Are you doubting me this far into our relationship?"

"Nope, not me. I wouldn't dream of it," Cassandra told her cousin innocently.

"Good. Sending you those names now, but I don't have addresses yet. The first guy did give one, but following it would put him in the middle of the East River," she said. "Unless we're dealing with a comic book hero, that just isn't possible," she told Cassandra.

"Agreed, but send me anything you do have. I'll make sense of it as we go along. When were these two photos taken?" she asked Valri.

"As near as I can place it, about a couple of years apart. I'm still working on connecting other people who might have been associated with your missing hunks."

"Come again?" Cassandra asked.

"It has to have hit you by now," Valri said. "All these dead guys could have been used in an old-fashioned movie about gorgeous guys. Maybe even singing and dancing ones," she added with a laugh.

Cassandra exchanged looks with Danny. In typical Valri fashion, the computer wizard had put her finger directly on the most salient point, the main connecting factor.

Chapter 15

"Well, actually it did," Cassandra said to the computer technologist. "I just didn't want to sound as if I was being shallow."

"Nothing shallow about being accurate," Valri told her. "To my way of thinking, I'd say that this is a very unique case," the Aurora Police Department's computer wizard said. "Okay, I'm in the process of exploring more names. Right now, there's just the two of these guys—and maybe not even that many," she said, still entertaining the possibility that this was one and the same man.

"Why would you say that?" Cassandra asked her cousin, wanting to explore Valri's thinking.

"Because these two guys look eerily alike, and as far as I can tell, they were never captured at the same time in the same place. I find that a little bit suspicious, but I could be totally wrong. However," Valri said, continuing on, "I haven't given up. There still might be more offenders on the list. Plus, these two could just look eerily alike.

"If there are any breakthroughs," Valri said, "I'll get back to you immediately."

"I'll be waiting," Cassandra told her cousin. "Meanwhile, please say hi to the rest of the family for Travis and me."

"Will do," Valri promised. And with that, the call ended.

Cassandra turned off her cell phone and put it away. She turned her attention back to Danny. "Call in your troops, and let's see if either one of these two guys can be found in the greater New York area," she told the detective. "I think it might be time to hit the bricks instead of sitting here and breathing in all this dust."

"Hit the bricks?" he echoed. "Is this an old Humphrey Bogart movie?" he asked, amused. He raised his hand as she began to answer him. "Doesn't matter. You're not going to get an argument out of me. Though I myself prefer Jerry Orbach in the original *Law & Order.*"

"That works for me too," Cassandra said.

"Like him, I actually prefer talking to people one on one," he told her.

Cassandra looked at him in surprise, but if he noticed, he gave no indication. He just continued with his explanation. "Looking into their eyes helps me see just how honest—or dishonest—they are being."

"Well, we certainly agree on that too," she told the detective. "I like hitting the bricks. A lot better than I like sitting in an office, pushing papers around and getting cross-eyed." She looked down at the address of one of the two suspects that Valri had given her. "Let's see what Rick Allen has to say about his friendship with Pete Wilson and if he has any feelings about the man disappearing the way that he suddenly did ten years ago."

They found Rick Allen at home. The man lived in a one-bedroom walk-up that had seen far better days but was not as run-down as it could have been. From all indications, Rick Allen hadn't been able to hold a steady job since Pete Wilson had abruptly disappeared the way he had.

Suspicious at first of the two detectives' appearance on his doorstep, it soon became obvious that he was more than happy to talk about the missing man he claimed was his best friend.

"I can't tell you what a great heart Peter had. Maybe a little too great," Allen said sadly.

"Could you tell us what you mean by that?" Cassandra asked.

Rather than answer her question directly, Rick Allen seemed to only want to talk to Danny. "Well, if you ask me, Peter was far too trusting," he told the New York detective. "He felt that he could tell everyone anything and that they would be receptive of his words and honest in their response," Peter Wilson's so-called friend stressed.

"I kept telling him that someday he would wind up regretting being so damn trusting. Hell," Rick Allen said, frowning at the memory, "this is the big city, not some little farm in the countryside."

"According to our information," Cassandra told the older man, referring to her notes, "your friend was born and bred right here in the heart of New York City."

Rick Allen frowned darkly at her, then went back to looking at the detective who had come to conduct the interview with her. It was obvious that Allen preferred Danny, but this often happened in interviews with witnesses or persons of interest.

"That doesn't change the fact that Peter was way too trusting," he told her gruffly, then turned his attention back to Danny.

For a moment, Cassandra was about to say something about keeping a civil tongue in his head. But then she decided there was nothing to be gained by putting this bitter older man in his place or on the defensive. Not to mention, her role was to listen, observe and ask questions, not scold.

The man's behavior just gave her that much more insight into his character.

"Did you ever talk to him about that?" she asked. "About his being so trusting?"

Rick Allen avoided making any eye contact with

her. Instead, he shifted his eyes to look at Danny and gave his answer to him, as if it had been Danny who had put the question to him.

"I did," the man admitted. "Once—but I didn't want him to think that I was picking on him," Allen said with what passed for an innocent expression. "I got the feeling that it was hard enough for Peter to make ends meet and to just go about the business of living. I did lend him money, and very honestly, I didn't expect to ever see it again.

"After a while," Allen said, "I began to notice that he kept looking over his shoulder, as if he expected someone to just come pouncing out of the shadows and overtake him. Maybe even wind up beating him up."

Danny took his cue from the fact that Rick Allen was addressing his words exclusively at him. Glancing at Cassandra and mentally apologizing to the woman, the New York detective pushed ahead and asked, "Why do you think that he would he expect that?"

"Because we've got a serial killer loose in the city—or so the rumor goes," Rick said whimsically. It was hard judging by his expression whether he bought into that or not.

At this point, Cassandra couldn't help herself. She had to ask the man. "Are you afraid of a serial killer?"

He spared her a look and snapped, "No." Then shifted to look at the very handsome detective before him.

"Why should I be?" he asked Danny. "It's probably all just a wild rumor that's been blown out of proportion."

"Bodies have been known to turn up," Danny said. He couldn't help pointing this out to the man.

"Hell, this is the big city. Bodies have been known to turn up all over the place," he told Danny with bravado. He went on to say, "Here. In Chicago. In Los Angeles. Hell, in any big city where people can get into an argument. But that still doesn't mean that there's a serial killer on the loose."

He laughed to himself, dismissing the idea. "If there was, I'd move back to my dad's farm and then just wait around to die of boredom."

Cassandra read between the lines and raised her eyes to look at the man who was talking. "I take it that you didn't like working on the family farm too much?"

"No longer than I had to," Rick answered honestly. "The second I could take off, I did," the man said, informing Danny proudly. "I didn't belong in the sticks. I was always meant to be where the action was."

He sat up straighter, his body language signaling that the interview was over, at least as long as the woman was here as well. He looked at Danny pointedly. "Is there anything else I can tell you?"

"No, not now," Danny answered. "If we think of anything, we'll get back to you."

Rick looked directly into Danny's eyes as he said,

"I'll be sure to keep a candle burning in the window for you."

Cassandra walked out of the apartment first, moving quickly. She was eager to get a breath of fresh air, such as it was.

Danny joined her, and they walked down the metal stairs to the street. Only then did she trust her voice not to carry up to the man they had just left. She thought he might have been listening to anything they said to one another. He struck her as that type.

"I think someone has a crush," she said, glancing back mischievously. The man seemed to have strong opinions about her. It said a lot.

Danny shook his head. "Hey, if it helps move the case forward, I'm okay with that."

Cassandra nodded. "It's interesting. While sitting there, I had a hard time picturing Rick Allen as someone's son," she replied, barely stifling the shiver that had come over her. "Because of my large family, I usually envision people as being part of a family, large or small. But not this guy," she said with feeling. "He just makes me want to shiver. Like there's a creepy story there."

The NYPD detective laughed, then surprised her by agreeing with her assessment. "Yeah, me too," Danny said, then asked, "Are you up to trying to find and talk to the other potential suspect that your resident computer genius unearthed?" He glanced at her over his shoulder as he led the way back to his vehicle.

"Absolutely," Cassandra told him with enthusiasm. She paused as she got into Danny's car. "Maybe it's just my imagination, but I feel like this case is *finally* moving—hopefully in the right direction."

Starting up his vehicle, the detective smiled at Cassandra. "I really hope that you're right," he told her. And then he began driving. "I think your cousin managed to locate what looked like a current address for this guy who befriended the second victim on the list."

"Valri is very good at her job. She knows how to dig deep in places others might miss. I've never known her to make a mistake," she told the detective proudly. Cassandra watched as the streets went by and realized that she hadn't answered his question yet. "Let's go," she said.

He paused at the next light. "There's just one problem," Danny told her.

"Just one?" she said, kidding, then immediately realized that he was being serious. "What's the problem?"

He blew out a breath. He was definitely not happy about this, but he knew he had to own up to it.

"The place is listed as being off the island," he told her, then said, "I'm going to need to get directions."

"From me?" she asked him, completely caught off guard.

"No," Danny corrected. "From the GPS system that's attached to the dashboard." He pointed toward it. "It's positioned so that I can't readily make it out, and I don't want to fiddle with it. Just put in the address and read the directions to me."

"Won't the GPS give you a readout?" she asked. All the systems she knew of talked.

"It would if the volume hadn't somehow gone dormant and then shorted out," he told her.

She didn't understand. "Can't you just replace it?"

His brow furrowed. "I can and I will, but that doesn't do me any good right now, does it?"

The truth of it was that he meant to upgrade the GPS, but more important things got in the way. He hated that she noticed his subpar system and realized that he had snapped the answer. He immediately toned it down a little. "I know my way around this city—just for some reason, not in the particular neighborhood where this guy's apartment is located," he confessed. "So," he began again, "if you don't mind…"

"Nope, I don't mind at all," she told him cheerfully, looking down at the GPS as she typed in the address that was written in on the sheet. "You ready?" she asked.

"Yeah, I'm ready."

Cassandra noticed that the New York detective's voice was rather strained, but she ignored it.

Getting to where Roy Adams lived was a challenge. They drove to a secluded part of Brooklyn, in a neighborhood that was more residential, with gardens and patches of grass that could pass as a lawn. The gray winter light barely peeked through the clouds. Because some people had cars parked on the streets, parking was especially difficult.

Finding the man was even more challenging.

Luckily, both he and Cassandra had good eye-sight and the determination to find Roy Adams. They knocked on doors and found a couple of his neighbors in, but no one had any idea where the man was.

Cassandra and Danny spent the rest of the day attempting to track Roy Adams down. They went into stores and showed pictures of him, even stopped people on the street. After a while, they sat in a café to regroup and go down another list of streets they could canvas. In the end, they got nowhere.

It was, Cassandra thought, as if they had used up their luck just by locating Rick Allen. Trying to find Roy Adams was a futile expedition.

When they went back to one of the neighbors who hadn't been there a few hours earlier, they struck potential gold. Lucy Valdez, a grandmother of three who worked as a nurse in a nearby hospital, suggested that the man was away, fishing. It was his favorite pastime, she confided.

"It's the middle of winter," Cassandra protested, pointing that out to the woman who had offered that excuse. The idea of fishing in what amounted to bitter cold had little to recommend it.

"Roy says, that way, he doesn't have to put up with any competition," the woman at the door informed them. She looked over her shoulder as she heard sizzling noises coming from the direction of her kitchen.

"Look, I gotta go. I'm starting my dinner late," she complained.

Not waiting for any response from the duo standing in her doorway, the woman closed it on them.

Cassandra exchanged looks with the frowning detective at her side. "I think that's our cue to call it a night. Are people here always this friendly?"

Danny chuckled. "They don't want to get involved. Mrs. Valdez has enough on her plate than to find herself wrapped up in a bunch of homicide cases."

"I get it. But still, we've gotta find this guy."

Cassandra nodded, totally in agreement. The more time they spent together, the more he knew he would miss her when she went back to California. They'd had this easy way of working together, as if they'd been on cases before. It only seemed natural to continue into the night. "You want to grab some dinner?"

Cassandra realized that she was hungry and had been for a few hours now. All that walking around fired up her appetite. "You've twisted my arm," she told the detective.

"What would you like?" he asked Cassandra.

She smiled at him as they returned to his vehicle again. Cassandra slid into her seat. "Oh, I don't know. Why don't you surprise me?"

A thought flashed through his mind that had nothing to do with dinner or anything remotely practical like that.

Surprise her, he caught himself thinking. How he wanted to just lean over and kiss her again, right here in the middle of nowhere after a long day. The idea seemed natural to him, to look into her flashing green eyes and draw her closer.

This time, it took a great deal of concentrated effort on his part to rein in his thoughts and focus on something other than bringing her exceedingly tempting mouth up to his.

It was not easy.

"You in the mood for Chinese food?" Danny finally asked her.

"I'm in the mood for food," she responded. "Anything but three-day-old dirt at this point will do nicely."

He looked at her as he brought his car into a nearly packed parking lot that accommodated three restaurants. "That is an interesting choice of food."

"Just my way of letting you know that I'm up for anything," she told him.

He nodded. "I got that impression," he said. Stopping his vehicle in a small parking space, he got out first. It was really cold out.

Danny turned up the collar on his coat. Without thinking, when Cassandra got out, he put his arm around her back to keep the chill at bay as best he could.

"Walk quickly," he recommended. "The restaurant door is just up ahead."

"And here I was planning on dawdling," she responded with a laugh.

"You really are a wise guy, you know that?" he said to her.

Cassandra smiled up into his face, completely amused despite the bitter cold night. She could feel herself responding to him.

"I know," she answered.

He walked faster to get Cassandra in through the restaurant's door as quickly as possible.

As he did so, Danny noticed that the California detective kept up without any complaint.

When they walked in, the warmth inside the restaurant all but embraced them.

It was an exceedingly welcome feeling.

Chapter 16

"I had no idea I was that hungry," Cassandra said, looking down at her empty plate. A plate that had been more than full just a little while ago with the most delicious orange chicken, sticky rice and stir-fried broccoli. They still had a great deal of food they could take home. Home. How easy it was to think of them together. Understandable, since they'd been working together every minute since they'd met. But disturbing too since she started to imagine how much it might hurt to leave.

She made sure to take mental pictures of Danny, how cute he was, especially now, when he was at ease, smiling and talkative.

Danny wiped his mouth, crumpled up his napkin and allowed it to drop down onto his own empty plate.

"You just got caught up in the case," he told her, supplying her with an excuse. "I've had the very same thing happen to me on more than one occasion. So," he continued, his eyes meeting hers, "do you want anything else?"

Cassandra paused for a moment, then told him, "No."

"If it wasn't so cold out, I would suggest a short walk to help kick-start digestion—we did have a lot to eat," Danny said, commenting on the portions they had just consumed. "But it really is pretty cold outside, so taking a walk, even a brisk one, isn't such a good idea." He grinned as he looked around for their server. Spotting her, he signaled for the check.

The waitress came over almost instantly and cheerfully handed them their bill. Glancing at the total, Danny proceeded to peel off a nice-sized tip to place on top of the bill, then left what amounted to the exact amount of the check to pay for their dinner.

"We'd wind up being popsicles before we ever managed to walk a couple of city blocks," he told her, returning to what he had mentioned earlier.

Walking out of the restaurant, his eyes met hers. "Unless you're interested in giving it a shot," the detective added as a postscript. His indication was that he would if she would.

Cassandra pulled her coat more tightly around herself. "Maybe tomorrow," she suggested, stifling a shiver.

His lips curved. "Tomorrow it is," he responded.

"As for now, I think that I'd better get you over to the hotel."

Despite the hour, Cassandra realized that she didn't really feel like calling it a night just yet.

"Do you live close by?" she asked as she got into his car.

The question surprised him. "Close enough," he answered. Because everyone knew how pricey apartments so close to the heart of the city were, he felt he needed to explain why he had gotten so lucky.

"The apartment I live in belonged to the former detective who initially recruited and trained me. Stan Beal was a lifelong bachelor who went to live in Florida when he retired. He hated to see his apartment go to waste, and he didn't want to sell it, so his solution was to pass it on to me as a 'relative,'" he told her with a smile. "Stan was a real good guy." "Why?" he found himself asking in response to her initial question about the closeness of his apartment.

"No reason," she answered. "I just thought I'd like to see it, that's all."

"It's not all that exciting," he told her. It was actually rather drab by modern concepts.

Cassandra shrugged noncommittally. "I just haven't seen all that much of New York City except for the precinct and the hotel—and interviewing witnesses."

"And you want to go sightseeing," Danny guessed.

"Eventually," she agreed. "But right now, I just want to see something that isn't part of the case."

He laughed softly. "Never exactly thought of my apartment as much of a tourist draw," he teased, "but you're more than welcome to come by and see it."

With that, he pulled away from the curb and drove to the apartment he had inhabited ever since his mentor had retired and taken off for Florida.

The detective's one-bedroom apartment, truly in the heart of Manhattan and not too far from the police station, was located on the fourth floor of a well-maintained prewar building. With only seven floors and five apartments per floor, it was the kind of residence where everyone knew each other's business—in the best possible way. Danny often found plates of cookies on his doorstep from one of his more grandmotherly neighbors. Now if only he could find someone to clean his apartment, he'd be in a better place to entertain visitors.

Unlocking the door, he switched on the light and immediately began to apologize. "Sorry, I wasn't expecting company," he explained as he moved about, picking up papers and cast-off clothing from the floor, stacking them together in a semblance of a pile on a love seat.

She grinned at the detective's apology. "No judgment," she said, trying to assure him. She looked around again and then smiled. "This is actually neater than the way my brothers lived until they found the loves of their lives, who accepted them 'for better or for worse.' Housekeeping fell under 'for worse.'"

His thoughts going back in time, Danny laughed softly to himself. "If she were here, my mother would have told you that she raised me better than that."

"She probably did, but right now you're as caught up as the rest of us are in this ongoing serial killer saga. Neatness has to take a back seat for the time being," she told him. "Trust me on that."

She was being awfully nice about this. A lot of women he knew would have been rather critical about the state of his living quarters, he thought. He rather liked the fact that she had given him a pass on his limited housekeeping abilities.

The more he got to know this unusual woman, the more he found to like. He couldn't help wondering if it was the ongoing case that was doing it—or if it was the woman.

Danny had a feeling that it was the latter since, sadly, this was not the first serial killer case he had worked on.

He gestured toward his kitchen. "Can I get you something to drink?" he offered. He knew that if he extended the offer to include something to eat, she might very well explode. He was pretty much stuffed to the gills himself.

"Do you have any diet soda?" she asked him. He didn't look like the type who favored diet drinks, much less anything carbonated, but she thought it was worth a shot.

"No alcoholic beverage?" he questioned.

She shook her head. "Not right now," she said. "I'd fall asleep right where I'm sitting."

"Can't have that," he told her. Walking over to his refrigerator, he opened the door and rummaged around for a moment. "You're in luck," he told her. "There's one unopened can left."

Taking it out, he offered the can to Cassandra. He fully expected her to pass on it, but to his surprise, she took it from him and popped open the top. A small fizzle showered down lightly for just a second.

Danny watched the woman close her eyes as she took a sip, savoring the drink. He found himself captivated for a moment.

"Never saw anyone enjoy soda quite like that," he told her.

She flushed just a little. "It's a guilty pleasure. Left to my own devices, I would probably drink four or five cans a day. I've had to cut back drastically in the last few years," she said.

"Never exactly thought of drinking soda as an indulgence," he said. He'd seen a lot of people on the force abuse alcohol, but diet soda never fell into that category. Every now and then, he liked a soda, but it wasn't his go-to, beverage.

She laughed. "I suppose it had something to do with the amount I consumed—it could have filled a small ocean at one point," she said.

Danny wound up shaking his head. "You really are a revelation, Detective Cavanaugh," he told her, amused.

"Glad I could entertain you," she told him as her eyes met his.

Cassandra had no idea exactly how they had come to be sitting so close to one another. And how that close proximity managed to stir her up the way that it did.

She could feel her pulse speeding up—just like her heartbeat.

I need to be careful, Cassandra thought, silently lecturing herself. Otherwise, she had a feeling she would wind up going a step too far.

But even as she issued that warning to herself, Cassandra could feel the effects that the detective's blue eyes were having on her, could feel herself growing warmer than the temperature warranted.

It didn't really help matters any to have the man take a sip from the can she was holding. Nor did it help to have him slowly run the tip of his thumb along her lips.

Cassandra swallowed. She was growing progressively hotter and could have sworn she heard a rushing noise in her ears.

Breathing took effort.

Cassandra hardly remembered Danny removing the can from her hand and placing it on the coffee table before them. What she found herself suddenly aware of was the detective leaning forward, taking her face in his hands and then softly pressing his lips against hers.

Her heart suddenly slammed against her ribs, completely stealing away her ability to breathe. Cassandra hardly remembered the detective taking her into his arms.

All she was really aware of was the end effect.

And the fact that everything inside of her was reduced to a single puddle.

The next moment, Cassandra caught herself returning the handsome detective's kiss. Over and over again, her mouth slanted over his, each kiss growing more ardent, more passionate. And each and every time she did, the fire within her only grew more.

Danny pulled her onto his lap, and she sat above him on the sofa. He kissed her with an intense passion he had no idea existed within him until it was suddenly there, dictating his every move.

But even so, he drew back just for a moment. "Are you sure you want to do this?" he asked her in a quiet, husky voice. The last thing he wanted was for her to feel as if the situation she found herself in had been forced.

Cassandra blinked, looking at him in slight confusion. "Are you trying to back out of this?" she asked the detective.

There was no way he wanted that, but he didn't want her feeling any sort of pressure either. "No, but—"

"Then shut up and kiss me, Detective," she told him. Without waiting for him to take his cue, she sealed her mouth to his.

The rest happened so quickly, it seemed as if it were all transpiring within the blink of an eye.

They did make it to the bedroom, but just barely. Clothes went flying in all directions, littering the floor and leaving them both nude and eager. Their bodies heated against one another, the flames rising higher and higher with every long, soulful kiss that passed between them as well as each long, loving caress.

Danny was eager to hurry through the lovemaking, to have the final moment explode within him and fill every empty, wanting crevice within his body. But at the same time, he wanted to savor every moment, to hold on to it and treasure every second he was experiencing, because it was so wondrously fulfilling.

Danny lovingly slid his hands over every curve, every tempting inch of her palpitating body.

Locked in a torrid embrace, he kissed Cassandra over and over again, each kiss growing more and more pronounced until he had her, willingly and eagerly moving beneath him, hungry for the wondrous feeling he seemed to be able to create within her.

When Danny finally entered her, Cassandra caught her lower lip between her teeth, stifling a cry. A soulful moan managed to escape, surrounding them.

United, they moved as one being, going faster and faster until the explosion overtook them, shaking them both down to their very souls.

And when it was over, they fell back, still wrapped in each other's arms, hardly able to draw in enough breath to sustain themselves.

She could feel her heart pounding against her rib-cage and thought it was never going to subside. But eventually, it did.

That was when she felt Danny looking at her. "What?" she questioned.

"I've got to admit, that was certainly a surprise," he told her, brushing his lips against her forehead.

"Why?" she asked, confused. "You didn't think I had it in me?"

"No," he laughed, drawing her closer to him, tucking his arm around her body again. "I didn't think that *I* had it in me," he told her. Danny kissed her forehead again. "No doubt about it, Cavanaugh," he said, lowering his voice. "You do bring out the very best in me. A 'best' I never even suspected I had."

A sparkle entered her eyes, teasing him. "Would you like to do it again?"

He could feel his heart beginning to race again as a smile curved his mouth. "Hell yes. But I think it's only fair to warn you, this time I just may expire."

She could only shake her head. "You do know how to turn a girl's head," she told him just before she brought her mouth up to his.

"I do my best," Danny answered, his warm breath teasing her just before he began to kiss her with every ounce of passion he had within him.

It was the man's third time around the block. With each pass that he made, the images he envisioned within his mind's eye grew more vivid, taking on form and breadth—and stoking what felt like a deep, inner rage within his chest. One that threatened to completely undo him.

This feeling was nothing new to him, but the extent to which it filled him was. He had never felt this intensity before.

He had found out about Danny Doyle and that little tramp's rendezvous in Doyle's apartment completely by accident. He had followed the detective's vehicle, waiting for him to be done with that little California witch and bring her back to the hotel.

He had even sat outside the restaurant in his car, waiting for them to be done and come out.

But instead of taking the woman and leaving her at her hotel, the detective had taken her to his place.

His place, damn it!

The very thought filled him with red-hot fury that he couldn't even put into words.

It made his blood boil.

They shouldn't be together, he thought darkly.

Doyle shouldn't be spending time with her. If anything, the detective should be giving *him* his attention. He had been cultivating the man for almost a year now, bringing him coffee just the way he liked it, finding topics of conversation that helped to make the detective's job more tolerable. He knew that for a fact.

That awful woman had no place being there with him, doing heaven only knows what.

He set his jaw hard. So hard he felt that it was close to snapping.

She'd pay for this, he promised himself. By God, that two-bit little whore was going to pay. He'd see to it.

He circled the building one last time, looking up to where he knew the detective's windows were located.

And then he made his way to his car and drove away.

Soon, he promised himself. He'd seize the opportunity for revenge very, very soon.

Chapter 17

A new warmth had generated between them and continued to thrive even after the other night, but Cassandra and Danny were both determined not to allow that feeling get in the way of their working well together.

More importantly, not get in the way of their catching the serial killer they were pursuing and doing their best to bring to justice.

When they walked into the precinct the following morning, the first person they ran into was Danny's partner, Simon Lee.

When he saw them, the detective looked as if he were barely able to contain himself.

Danny was well acquainted with the signs. Something was definitely up, and by the look on his partner's face, it wasn't good.

"Okay, Lee, what's up?" the detective asked before he even took off his overcoat.

The man's eyes swept over the duo as the words fairly exploded from his mouth. "They found more bodies!"

Cassandra's heart sank. She might be in the business of solving murders, but she ached every time a person was killed. "When?" she asked.

"Half an hour ago," Danny's partner told them.

"Was it recent?" Danny asked. Just what had set this killer off on his latest killing spree, he couldn't help wondering.

"That's the odd part," Lee told them as he followed behind the pair into the squad room. "It looks like these people have been dead for about a year or so. The bodies were just taken into autopsy, so we'll know more once the ME gets done.

"It's like the killer has been saving them somewhere and then for some reason decided that now was the time to release them." Lee told them his theory. "The city is just catching up and coming back to life after experiencing a two-year paralyzing hiatus," he said, referring to what New York—and the whole world—had endured with the pandemic. "There's been a lot of construction going on all over the place in an effort to get back to normal." He shrugged, sitting down at his desk. "I guess no one noticed these bodies being planted."

"Or if they did, they pretended not to," Danny said, hanging up his overcoat as he shook his head.

The information was not computing as far as Cassandra was concerned. Taking off her own jacket, she blew out a frustrated breath.

"How can they do that?" she asked.

He knew she was referring to the fact that the citizens were deliberately trying to ignore what was going on right in front of them. But he could also see the other side of the picture.

"It's called survival," Danny told her.

"Maybe," Cassandra agreed. "But at what price?" To her, the people who cast a blind eye to what was happening were sacrificing their humanity.

"Why don't we get philosophical *after* we solve this mystery and catch this cold-blooded killer?" Lee suggested.

At bottom, Danny's partner was right, Cassandra thought. She caught her lower lip between her teeth as she tried to make sense out of all this.

"It's got to be someone who's in the heart of things. Someone who can easily blend in without being noticed or calling attention to himself," she said, thinking out loud.

Lee inclined his head, agreeing with the detective from California. "Kind of like 'Where's Waldo?' right?"

"Yes, except in this case, Waldo is a lot less friendly," Cassandra speculated, a deep frown transforming her features. She only wished this situation was like that lighthearted challenge, but it obviously wasn't. Waldo had never left a stack of bodies in his wake.

"How many bodies did they find?" Danny asked.

"I haven't seen them for myself," Lee admitted. "But I was told that there were three."

"All good-looking men between the ages of twenty to forty?" Cassandra guessed, mentally crossing her fingers that she was wrong about that this time.

Lee looked at her and sighed. This was definitely the work of the same person. "It's like you were there."

She blew out a frustrated breath. "Only in my nightmares," she told the two men. The fact that it was the same person doing the killing meant he was getting braver. Hopefully, he was also growing more careless since he hadn't gotten caught yet. "Can we go to autopsy?" she asked Danny.

"Not yet," Lee told her. "From what I heard, the medical examiner was just getting started, and she has a reputation of not liking having anyone looking over her shoulder until the autopsy is completed. So it's going to be a while."

"There are probably no surprises. I mean, it's got to be the same guy, right?" she asked, looking from one man to the other.

Danny nodded. "That's the option that gets my vote," he answered. "Do we know who these latest victims are?"

Another member of Danny's team, Eduardo Suarez, walked in just in time to hear him ask the last question. He had an answer for the team leader.

"We've managed to get IDs on them," Eduardo said as he joined the group. He had brought in three photographs and now hung them up on the bulletin board. "I've got to say that this guy's got great taste," he commented.

"For a crazy person," Travis said as he joined the group.

"They found three more bodies," Cassandra told her cousin.

"Yeah, I just heard," Travis replied. "Maybe the city can call a moratorium on construction for a while," he said.

She looked at Travis. He was joking, right? "You really think that's going to stop this guy from killing people?"

Travis shrugged. "Wishful thinking."

Cassandra turned toward Danny. They needed to get busy. "Where would you like us to start?" she asked him.

"We talk to the families if there are any in the area, try to reconstruct the dead men's lives. Working backwards, we'll focus on both the similarities and the differences in all three cases. Maybe that'll wind up pointing us in the right direction," he told the rest of his team. Several more members had walked into the squad room and had gathered around him.

Cassandra nodded, agreeing with Danny's assessment. "All we need is just one break," she told the others gathered around them.

"That's good in theory," Lee told her. "But…" His voice trailed off.

She knew where Danny's partner was going with this. "I know, I know," she agreed. "We need to make that theory a reality."

She definitely didn't want to step on Danny's toes, especially after the night they had spent together, so she proceeded with utter caution, taking nothing for granted. "What do you want us to do?"

Danny distributed the copies of the photographs of the latest victims who had been discovered. He gave one to each of member of his team, including Cassandra.

"Go talk to the dead men's friends, employers, landlords—anyone who might have seen them before they disappeared off the face of the earth," he instructed. "The serial killer has to have quirks we can track down and use. Something that can pinpoint him, however small and initially insignificant," he told his team. "It's only hidden from us at the moment because we can't see it."

That sounded like a saying, Cassandra thought. Unable to help herself, she asked, "Can I embroider that on a towel?"

"You can do anything you want once we catch this SOB. Until that happens, I want all of our attention to be directly centered on this guy." His eyes swept over the people on his team, taking each and every one of them into account. "Have I made myself clear?"

A sea of heads bobbed up and down. "Absolutely," several members told him.

Another one gave him a smart salute. "You got it."

"Uh-huh," another member responded.

Danny looked over toward Cassandra. She hadn't responded yet. "Detective Cavanaugh?" he asked, waiting for her answer.

"You were never clearer, Detective Doyle," she said to him cheerfully as her eyes met his.

"Then let's get to work," Danny said, encouraging his team.

The distinct squeak of the mail cart as the delivery clerk made his way through the squad room seemed particularly grating on her nerves this morning.

Cassandra paused what she was working on and looked up to find Curtis Wayfare approaching their work area.

She could see the look on the clerk's face as he pushed the mail cart in front of him. He was looking in Danny's direction. Cassandra could see the man's features softening.

The man was seriously interested in Danny, Cassandra thought. Whether it was just a harmless man crush or something more remained to be seen.

When his glance shifted toward her, for just a second, she felt a really cold shiver zip down her back. Maybe it was just her imagination, but even so, she couldn't shake the feeling that the mail clerk just didn't like her. She was more than a little convinced that for whatever reason, the man was harboring a strong grudge against her.

"I hear that more bodies turned up, Detective," Wayfare said, directing his words toward Danny. "Think it's the same killer?" Wayfare asked him. He appeared to be genuinely interested in Danny's opinion. He also sounded as if the conversation was just between the two of them, excluding the others in the room.

"They did," Danny answered, keeping his tone matter-of-fact sounding. Then, because he felt it was warranted, he added, "The ME will undoubtedly be able to tell us if it's the same serial killer."

"I bet it is." The clerk almost sounded cheerful as he made the pronouncement. "Some puzzle, eh, Detective?" Wayfare spared a glance in Cassandra's direction. His smile faded almost completely, and then the clerk resumed his route. "Well, good luck, Detective Doyle. I've got mail to deliver. Call me if you need anything. I'm working a full day today. Just like you," he added happily.

Squeaky wheels marked his departure.

Cassandra said nothing until Wayfare had left the area on his way elsewhere. The clerk sent shivers down her spine and it was not the welcomed kind, she couldn't help thinking.

"You know, if I were you," she told Danny, "I'd make sure that my sidearm was always on my person."

Danny looked at her. "You mean because of Curtis Wayfare?" he asked her. "Oh, the guy's harmless enough."

"If you say so," Cassandra responded. It was obvious that she didn't agree with the detective. "But there's something about the way he looks at you that would definitely give me pause if I were you."

Danny waved a hand at her statement. "Curtis is just grateful. When he first came here about two years ago, he was like a lost puppy. I felt sorry for the guy, so I just spent a little time with him, pointed him in the right direction. He's been thankful ever since." Danny raised his shoulders in an absent-minded shrug. "That's all."

"Uh-huh. And here I thought that you New Yorkers were supposed to have been born suspicious."

He laughed and shook his head. "We just have a bad reputation. Who knows how it started. You won't find nicer people than in this city, especially in a crisis—of which we've had many."

Cassandra nodded her head and smiled. He was so cute, the way he defended his city. She understood the impulse since she loved her home fiercely. Aurora had sheltered her, had revived her after painful assignments and had shown her the meaning of love and family. She could never leave the Cavanaugh kingdom, even though this handsome detective had her thinking traitorous thoughts.

She watched him browsing through folders and

notes. And then he looked up suddenly, directing his gaze at her. "I think I just found something."

"What?" she asked, trying to direct her vision toward what he was looking at.

"This must have gotten mixed in with the wrong papers," he commented, holding up a page. "It's information on your cousin."

Wayfare was immediately forgotten, and renewed interest about the case they were dealing with entered her eyes. "What kind of information?" She guided her chair in closer to Danny's in order to get a better look at what he had found.

"It says here that just before he disappeared, Nathan intended to apply to the police force. That he was no longer interested in leading an aimless life but had decided to make something of himself—like the rest of his family. He was planning on taking a police aptitude test and had high hopes he was going to do well."

"And?" she prodded, hoping there was more to it.

"And nothing," Danny told her. "There's nothing more in the folder or on the misplaced page I found stuffed inside. There's nothing more about your cousin at all," he said. He turned the page, examining it more closely and thumbing through other pages but didn't find anything else.

She looked at the page. There was no more information to be gleaned from it, "We don't know how he did," she said sadly.

"We don't even know *if* he did," Danny said.

"There's no official mention of his taking a test to get into the police academy or anything like that."

"Is there any way we can find out if he did take the exam to get into the police academy?" she asked.

"The papers regarding that might have been warehoused," Danny suggested.

"Warehoused?" Cassandra echoed, immediately interested. "Warehoused where?"

"It's an old building located downtown," he told her. "If I remember correctly, it's by the river," he told her.

"Can we get into the building and access those old files, or would we need to have someone's permission to get us in?" Cassandra wanted to know. She followed that by making the detective understand why she was pushing this the way she was. "I know that my Uncle Brian wants to bury this heretofore missing family member in the family plot.

"It would just make him feel better," Cassandra explained. "I get the impression that he feels guilty about what happened to Nathan. That if he hadn't lost touch with him, then maybe he would still be alive."

Danny shook his head. "There's no point in the man beating himself up for that," Danny told her. "From what you said, your cousin's mother wanted to cut off all ties to the family."

"She did," Cassandra said, and confirmed with a sigh. "But Brian Cavanaugh is the chief of detectives. He takes *everything* upon himself. The only thing I can do to make things somewhat easier on his conscience is to at least solve the riddle of what happened to Nathan after Uncle Brian lost track of him."

Moved, Danny nodded. "Okay, let me see what I can do," he told her, heading for his captain's office.

"Want me to come with you?" Cassandra offered. She was already half out of her chair and rising to her feet.

But Danny shook his head, putting his hand up to stop her. "No, you stay here. When it comes to the captain, I really do better when I approach him on my own."

Cassandra smiled as she inclined her head toward the detective. "I bow to your wisdom," she told him.

He paused for a moment, waiting for the inevitable punch line that he felt was going to be coming.

Danny was really surprised when it didn't. He decided not to make any sort of a reference to that effect. He saw it as progress on her part.

"I'll be right back," Danny said, leaving the squad room quickly.

"I'll be here," she said to the detective with a resigned sigh. After a moment, she got back to looking over the folders that were spread out on the desk she was using.

Chapter 18

Cassandra would read a couple of words or so—none of which had any sticking power when it came to her brain—and then look up, waiting for the door at the far end of the squad room to open again.

But it didn't.

Doyle was taking a lot of time to talk to his captain. Maybe the man didn't want to be convinced.

And then, finally, the door opened again. Cassandra gave up all pretense of reading the file before her. Getting up, she crossed over toward the detective.

"So, what did the captain say?" she asked the second that she was within the detective's earshot. "Will he release my cousin's body and have it sent back to my uncle?"

He hated to disappoint her, but he wasn't about

to lie. "Not yet, but soon," Danny said quickly as he saw her expression fall. "The captain wants to give it a little more time. He feels that we might be on the brink of getting some answers."

For once, Cassandra found that she had to dig deep to find some optimism. She sighed. "I hope that he's right and something comes of this."

"I've known the captain for a while now, and while he's not the world's friendliest man, he does have good instincts and is usually more right than not about things," Danny said. "And no," he added with a small laugh, "In case you're wondering, I'm not wired."

She looked at him in surprise. Why would she even think that? This was not an overly trusting bunch of detectives, she decided.

"That never even crossed my mind," Cassandra told him. She sighed again, looking down at the file she had been going through. "I am getting cross-eyed from reading and rereading these files, trying to find the one salient point that I might have missed before. The one thing that might wind up pointing us to the killer."

Danny frowned, looking at the folder she was reading. "If it's even there."

"It *has* to be," Cassandra said, insistent. "The guy's human, and all humans have a habit of slipping up somewhere along the line. Some more often than others, but they all do it," she told him. "We just have to be patient and find just where this guy made a mistake."

She had an idea. Cassandra pulled out the two photos she had had blown up—the two that Valri had forwarded to her phone—and placed them side by side. They were as clear as possible but still fuzzy.

"Maybe we can try to locate some of the remaining friends or relatives of the serial killer's victims. One of them might remember seeing one of these guys lurking around our victims, trying to spend time with them," she said hopefully.

"It's definitely worth a try," Lee agreed. "We're not getting anywhere this way," he said needlessly.

Danny pulled up the list he had put together on his computer. He didn't need to count them. The names were imprinted on his mind. "All told, we've got fifteen victims."

"There might be more," Lee said to his partner.

Danny closed his eyes for a moment as he sighed, searching for patience. It was in precious short supply—even less than usual. "I realize that, but let's focus on the ones we know about at the moment," he said, instructing his partner.

Lee nodded. "How many is that?"

"Not nearly enough to answer our questions," Danny told the man, less than happy about the results.

Cassandra drew the sheet of paper closer to her. "All it takes is just one," she said, staring at the names on the list as if doing that would somehow emboss them on her brain. "Question is, which one is it?" she murmured to herself, looking at the list of names and the photos that went with them.

Nothing stood out or spoke to her. But then, that was to be expected.

"Let's see how many of these people are still living in the immediate area, or at least the state," Cassandra said, thinking that was as good a place as any for her to start.

As it turned out, there were nine friends or relatives of the deceased men still living somewhere in the general vicinity. One had moved to Manhattan, while the other eight were somewhere within the other four boroughs.

Cassandra began to grow hopeful again.

Danny split the names up, handing them out to his team. The accompanying words were not exactly brimming with hope, Cassandra couldn't help but notice.

"I really don't hold out that much hope of finding anyone who can wind up pointing us in the right direction," he told his team.

Second verse, same as the first, Cassandra couldn't help thinking. "I keep telling you, Detective, you need to think positive."

Danny sighed, doing his best not to let what she was saying get on his nerves. There was such a thing as baseless optimism.

"Okay," he agreed. "I'm *positive* that none of these

people are going to point us in the right direction." There was a slight edge to his voice.

"You really have to work on improving your attitude, Detective," she said.

"This *is* my improved attitude," he said to the woman.

All Cassandra could do at the moment was shake her head. She needed some fresh air, no matter how cold it felt going into her lungs. "Well, I'm going to go and interview my two people to see if there's anything they can tell me that'll point me in the right direction."

It was a long shot, but at least it was something, she thought.

A weary smile rose to his lips as Danny shook his head. "It never rains on your parade, does it, Cavanaugh?"

"Oh, sure it does," she said, contradicting him. "I just make sure to always keep an umbrella handy."

Danny caught himself laughing. "Let me see the two names that you have."

"Why?" she asked. Did he think she wouldn't be able to find the addresses? "I'm not going to get lost." She had a decent sense of direction, and she had also scrutinized online maps of the area. "Unlike you, I have a very sophisticated GPS."

Okay, maybe that was a low blow, but it irritated her that he would think she needed a chaperone. This wasn't nineteenth-century England—at least, she hoped it wasn't.

Some men she'd worked with felt she needed constant protecting. More than once, she'd had to explain that her training had been thorough and that she could take care of herself. Could Danny be another obstacle in her path to solving this case?

"That's not what I'm worried about," he told the woman from Southern California. "I just figured that we can combine our lists and go question these people together."

Her first thought was that he wanted to hide his feeling that she couldn't hack it as a detective. He didn't want to be liable if anything happened to her while chasing down this killer. She could feel her back going up. "You know that I can take care of myself."

"I know. I was just worried about the people you're going to be questioning," Danny told her with a wink. "Besides, I figure that two sets of eyes and ears are always better than just one."

She was not about to waste precious time arguing with the detective. If this was the way he wanted to play it, so be it. She couldn't shake the feeling that they couldn't afford to lose more time than they already had.

A gut feeling had taken hold, driving that point home. The kind of gut feeling that her uncles and occasionally her cousins like to talk about having.

The kind that she instinctively knew she couldn't afford to ignore. She couldn't explain the feeling; she only knew that if she ignored it, she might very well wind up regretting it.

"Fine, we'll join forces. You'll probably strike fear into their hearts, and we'll get our answers—if there are any answers to get," she added, thinking about what he had said earlier.

He looked at Cassandra in surprise. "You're not arguing with me?"

The smile that curved her lips was an amused one. "I get the feeling that in this case, arguing with you wouldn't do me any good. Besides," she said, not able to help herself, "if I was intent on opposing you, I wouldn't tell you. I'd just do it and let the pieces fall where they may."

"Now you have me worried," the detective said, only half kidding.

An easygoing grin quirked her mouth as a smile entered her eyes. "Sorry, that wasn't my intent."

The hell it wasn't, Danny thought. Just when he felt he finally had a handle on the woman, she threw a curve at him. It was obvious that she liked keeping him on his toes. To be honest, he couldn't really say that it bothered him.

He had a genuine question for her. "You want to call these people first, or just surprise them?"

Cassandra was startled that Danny gave her a choice in the matter rather than doing something that he had decided was set in stone.

She gave him an honest answer. "I've always had better luck with surprises."

Danny, on the other hand, liked to have things as predictable as possible. But he supposed he could see the advantage on having surprise on his side. For now, he nodded his head.

"All right," he said agreeably, "then surprise it is."

Standing behind her as she sat at her desk, Danny indicated the list before her. "Pick one of the people on the list. We'll go see if we can find that person at home or maybe even at work."

Looking at the list, she printed out information on the first four people that were on it, then circled them.

Danny frowned a little as he took in the names of the places. "Isn't that biting off a bit more than you can chew?" he asked.

"We're not showing up at all these places. We have no way of knowing if we're going to find *any* of these people where they're supposed to be. I know all the names on the list were initially researched, but things do have a way of changing, not to mention that people do just pick up and move. This, at least, allows us to gather some sort of information about one or two of the victims." She turned in her chair. The detective was standing much too close and generating all sorts of feelings that had nothing to do with tracking people down. Her throat felt dry as she formed the words. "I'm just attempting to cover all our bases."

Danny nodded. "I get that and appreciate the way you're thinking." He moved back so that she could push her chair away from the desk and get to her feet. "Let's go."

The detective paused for a moment to tell his partner just where he and Cassandra were going.

"Detective."

Curtis Wayfare's deep voice called out just before Danny managed to reach the squad room door.

He recognized the voice. The detective stifled a sigh as he turned toward the man who had called to him.

The mail clerk pushed his cart toward the man he clearly seemed to idolize. Wayfare was holding out a coffee container. "You forgot to take your coffee with you."

Danny was caught off guard. "Oh, right. I did." The detective took the container from Wayfare. "Thanks."

The mail clerk was beaming at him, as if he had just done something really noteworthy as well as personal. "You know you have trouble functioning without coffee, Detective," Wayfare told him knowingly, as if their so-called friendship went way back.

"Yeah, thanks," Danny said to the mail clerk, feeling somewhat awkward for the first time in the man's presence. He looked at Cassandra. "Like I said, we'd better hit the road."

Wayfare paused and looked after the departing detective. "Good luck," the mail clerk called out. His attention was exclusively directed toward the New York detective.

Cassandra waited until the clerk was out of earshot. "Your fairy godmother must have oiled the wheels on his cart. I didn't hear him roaming around the squad room this time."

Danny's frown went clear down to the bone. "He's not my fairy godmother," the detective told Cassandra.

"Oh, I beg to differ. I think Wayfare certainly thinks he is," she contradicted. "I think he would have carried you into the elevator if you would have let him."

Danny's frown deepened. Her comment made him uncomfortable. "You're exaggerating, Detective," he said.

"You didn't see the way he looked at you. I would say that look is nothing short of idolizing you." She grew serious. "I don't know if you're just his hero, or if there's something else involved."

"Speak plainly," he said to the woman. "Are you suggesting that Wayfare is the serial killer?"

Danny didn't know whether to laugh or take her seriously.

"What I'm suggesting is that there are eight million people all crowded into this little island of a city, and who knows what some of these people might be capable of?" she said to Danny. "I just think that we should keep our options open.

"By the way," Cassandra said as they walked out to the elevator, "do you know anything about this mail clerk? What his background is, things like that?" A lot of questions popped up in her mind when it came to Wayfare.

"I know next to nothing about the man," Danny said admittedly. "The only time I pay any attention to him is when he comes squeaking in and drops off a piece of mail or a package on my desk."

She pushed the down button, waiting for the elevator to arrive. "His cart stopped squeaking," she said, "right after you made a comment about the noise the wheels made."

"Are you saying he did that for me?" he said in disbelief. "That was just a coincidence."

"All I'm saying is for you to keep your mind open to the possibility that he's trying to please you. At this point, we don't know why."

He looked at her as the elevator arrived, opening its doors. "I think we both could use some fresh air," he suggested. She was letting her imagination run away with her, he thought.

"In the city?" she questioned, barely hiding the grin that overtook her face.

At that point, Danny laughed. "You work with what you have."

Pressing for the ground floor, the detective waited until the car went down to its destination. When it reached the lobby, the elevator doors opened.

Danny waited to comment until they were leaving the building. "You're wrong, you know."

"About?" she asked, not really sure what the man was referring to.

"About the mail clerk."

"You mean Wayfare?" Cassandra said.

"Yeah, him. He probably thinks that being friendly with me might help him get a raise, or at least not laid off," he said.

Cassandra shrugged. "You might be right."

He looked at her before they reached his vehicle, making a judgment call. "But you don't think so."

"Right now, until proven otherwise, everyone is a suspect in my eyes," she said.

"And you seemed like such a trusting soul," Danny said with a laugh. He liked that underneath her cheerfulness lurked an aggressive and observant detective. How he felt sorry for future perpetrators who were caught by her. They didn't stand a chance. And neither did he, come to think of it.

She reached out and touched his shoulder, a quick and flirtatious impulse. It reminded him of the previous night, what they meant to each other for a few precious hours.

"You know, Danny, we're just as suspicious in Aurora, California, as you are in New York City. We're just better at hiding it. We smile more. Between you and me," she said, getting into his car and reaching for her seat belt, "that's how we wind up catching the bad guys—by acting as if we don't suspect them—until we're snapping the handcuffs on their wrists."

"Ah," he nodded, starting up his vehicle. Excitement brewed within him, and not just for solving this case. He began to think his feelings had everything to do with his budding infatuation for this California detective dynamo. "Mystery solved."

Chapter 19

"And you're looking into my cousin's background, why?" Denise Wilson, the woman standing in the doorway, asked. Less than thrilled about being questioned about her annoying cousin, she hadn't been quick about responding to the detective's urgent knocking on her door.

For her part, Cassandra was about to walk away when no one responded the third time around. But because he could faintly detect the sound of a TV, Danny was fairly certain that there was someone in the apartment. So he knocked again, more urgently this time.

When she pulled the door open a crack, the gray-haired, slightly disheveled woman did not look happy about being disturbed. Her eyes narrowed as she regarded these people with suspicion.

"What do you want?" she demanded in a less than friendly voice.

Danny immediately held up his badge and ID for her benefit. "We'd like a few words with you about your cousin, Ms. Wilson. Pete," the detective said.

The woman's face darkened. "Maybe later," she said, trying to close her door again.

Danny was not about to move. He kept his foot in the doorway so that the woman wasn't able to push it closed. "Now would be better," he told her in a no-nonsense voice.

"This will only take a minute," Cassandra said, attempting to soften the woman.

"Yeah, right." The woman rolled her eyes and sighed dramatically. "Oh, all right. C'mon in," she told the duo. But as she opened her door further to admit them in, she looked at her watch. "You got ten minutes," she said, putting them on notice. And then ordered, "Talk fast."

"No problem," Danny responded.

The entrance to the apartment was narrow and extremely cluttered. The woman was obviously a hoarder. Danny focused exclusively on the annoyed woman.

"Our records indicate that you're related to Pete Wilson," Danny said.

Denise Wilson appeared less than pleased about the connection. A thin, angular woman, she raised her chin defiantly as she asked the two detectives, "And you're looking into my cousin's background, why?"

"We're conducting a routine questioning," Danny informed her. "According to the information we've managed to gather, your cousin, Pete Wilson, was friends with Claude Jefferson, whose body was recently found intermingled with five other skeletons."

It was obvious that the woman had absolutely no intention of being helpful. "So?" Denise said in a challenging way.

"So," Danny continued, "we were wondering if you had ever heard the two of them arguing or having any sort of a disagreement."

She seemed almost insulted by the question. "Look, I've got better things to do than to hang around paying attention to who my cousin argues with. For your information," she said to the two detectives, "we don't even get together around the holidays." Her voice grew even colder. "Are we done?"

At this point, he saw no advantage in pushing the woman. Not until they had something to actually go on. "Unless you have anything to add, Ms. Wilson, I suppose we are," Danny told her. For now, this was going nowhere.

"No, I don't have anything to add," the woman answered, striking an almost antagonistic attitude. "Other than the fact that Pete thinks he's such a big deal, doing what he does." There was nothing but contempt in her voice. "Like that makes him special."

"And you don't think he's special," Cassandra concluded. A sliver of a premise occurred to her, and she focused on expanding it.

The woman glared at her, stunned by the question. "Special?" she repeated with more than a little contempt. "Have you *met* my cousin? He thinks he's such a big shot because he doesn't have to work if he doesn't want to."

"And why doesn't he have to work?" Danny asked. He hadn't gotten that impression when he examined the man's records. There wasn't all that much there. Still, he could have missed something.

"Because his parents died and left him a boatload of money, that's why," the woman said with contempt. It was more than obvious that she resented her cousin. "You'd think he would be happy—but he's not."

"Why isn't he happy?" Cassandra asked. Maybe they were finally getting somewhere, she thought, mentally crossing her fingers.

Denise Wilson shook her head as she shrugged. "Something about not giving him the true worth of his parents. They were both killed in a boating accident." She sighed, not about to elaborate any further. "If you ask me, I'd say that Pete was a little off, spouting gibberish." Her expression softened as she looked more closely at Danny. "My guess is that this is one case that isn't going to be solved for a very long time—if ever. But the good thing about wanting to solve a murder is that if you can't find the answers to one, there'll be another murder coming along soon enough."

And then Denise looked at her watch. "Looks like

you're out of time, detectives, and I've got some-where else to be," she announced.

In Cassandra's opinion, Denise Wilson looked far from dressed for any sort of an occasion. But she also didn't sound as if she were about to volunteer anything further at the moment.

Danny found that he had to struggle to hold on to his temper. He could feel himself on the verge of losing it and telling Wilson's cousin that she was de-liberately throwing up roadblocks, but that was not going to get them anywhere in their investigation. He had half a mind to take her into the precinct for further questioning. But for now, he let that go.

With effort, Danny stiffly thanked the woman for her time. She closed the door before he could get all the words out.

"And another friendly, concerned person heard from," he murmured. Taking Cassandra's arm, he left the building.

"Well, that was a depressing waste of time," Danny commented in disgust.

"That doesn't mean the next one will be," Cas-sandra told him, sounding a great deal more upbeat than he was.

Danny stopped for a moment as they approached his vehicle. "You really are optimistic, aren't you?"

"I have found that it's the only way to survive," she told him. "And the minute we get that serial killer off the street, all this running around will all turn out to be worth it."

Danny could only shake his head incredulously. A smile curved his lips. For a second, he was taken back in time. "My mother would have loved you."

Stunned, Cassandra looked at him in total wonder. "That has to be just about the nicest thing you've ever said to me," she told the New York detective.

Danny lifted his shoulders in a vague, dismissive shrug. "Guess I must be slipping." He spared her a glance as he unlocked his car. "So, are you game to question the next person on the list?" He wouldn't blame her if she wasn't.

But there wasn't a moment of hesitation on her part. "Absolutely," Cassandra told him with enthusiasm.

The next person they questioned was another one of Pete Wilson's acquaintances. Unlike the woman they had just spoken to, Dwight Jorgenson found Pete Wilson to be a very intriguing man.

Jorgenson had nothing but nice things to say about Denise Wilson's cousin, although their friendship did not go back very far. It seem to encompass only the last two years, roughly the space of time, it turned out, that Wilson had been working delivering mail at the precinct.

Cassandra realized that Valri had mentioned to her that a Pete Wilson had worked out at the same gym that her cousin had before both had just vanished. It seemed like an odd coincidence to her. Could this Wilson be the same person? Had he turned up again? She wanted to make sure before she ran any of this by Danny. She didn't want to look like a fool, jumping the gun.

"He's an avid bridge player," Jorgenson told them, then said, "I'm in awe of the way his mind works. It's like he's about twelve moves ahead at any given time—and a totally different person."

Danny exchanged looks with Cassandra. "What do you mean by 'different'?" he asked, unclear as to what the man was attempting to convey.

"Well, when I try to talk to him about anything else, he just reverts to single-word answers. Like he has no interest in anything that doesn't challenge his mind.

"You can tell the difference," Jorgenson said. "When you mention something that Wilson's keen about, you can see this light entering his eyes. Like he's suddenly come to life." Continuing, the man shrugged. "When he's not interested in something, it's like the power was suddenly shut off." Jorgenson looked frustrated. "I'm not explaining this very well."

"No," Cassandra contradicted, determined not to lose the man. "I think that you're explaining the situation *very* well. Most people at least pretend to listen or be accommodating to the other person. It sounds like Mr. Wilson was laser-focused on his own life and whatever interested him. Nothing else."

The fact that the man lit up like a Christmas tree was not wasted on Danny. Cassandra knew how to communicate with people, he thought, how to get them to talk.

She had turned out to be an asset.

They talked to two other people who knew or had known Pete Wilson at some point or other. Living in different parts of the city, it took a bit of doing to find them. It was telling that other than Wilson's cousin, the three people they found to talk to were all men. No women seemed to populate Wilson's inner sphere.

By the time Danny and Cassandra had finished questioning the second of the two people who knew this "Pete Wilson," it had grown dark.

It was definitely time to call it a day, Danny thought.

"Tomorrow is Saturday," Danny told her as he walked Cassandra back to his car. "And unless the captain calls us in for some reason, how would you like to play tourist?"

Cassandra looked at the man at her side in utter surprise. She wasn't sure that she had heard him correctly. "Are you offering to take me sightseeing, Detective? While we're in the middle of hunting down a serial killer?"

He inclined his head, a warm smile curving his mouth. He had never been one for going the tourist route. But suddenly, it was sounding very appealing.

"Sometimes, taking a break makes you think more clearly. So, are you interested?" he asked.

The wide smile on her face gave him his answer.

They stopped at her hotel room to pick up a change of clothes for her, then went on to his apartment, where they spent a glorious evening making one another forget that such things as serial killers existed and lived among normal, peaceful people, disrupting their lives whenever a whim moved them.

They made unabashed, reckless love on the bed they'd messed up the night before.

The second time around, Cassandra discovered, much to her surprise and happiness, it was even more glorious and exciting than the first time had been.

They lay side by side, breathing erratically and marveling at what adrenaline could do. Cassandra turned over on her side and stared at her partner in more than one arena.

"Let's pretend that this is our lives. Just this night and this bed."

There was a pause where Danny ran a hand through his hair. He then turned to face her and grinned. "I'm right with you on that."

His blue eyes glinted with mischief as he pulled her back to him and kissed her.

Eventually, exhaustion came to claim both of them, and they wound up falling asleep in each other's arms.

Still sound asleep, Cassandra felt something stirring beside her. Slowly opening her eyes, she realized that it was Danny. She felt lit up from the inside.

Sliding a finger lightly down her nose, he whispered, "Open your eyes, Cavanaugh. Time to wake up."

She struggled to clear her mind. It wasn't easy. Danny had managed to tire her out more than she had thought possible. She was still half asleep but oh so happy.

"Another body?" she murmured, asking the first thing that came to her mind as she dragged herself up into a sitting position. She desperately struggled to wake up.

"Right now, the only bodies around are yours and mine." He kissed her shoulder, sending arrows of warm desire shooting through her. "Time to get ready to go sightseeing," he told her, brushing his lips against hers. "This might be the only opportunity that you get to be able to do that. With the team picking up some of the questioning, we get a little break. Granted, there's too much to stuff into even a week, much less a day of sightseeing, but we'll give it our best shot," he promised. "You snooze, you lose."

The urge to sleep was beginning to slip away as the world around her came into focus. Cassandra blew out a breath.

"Then I'd better get ready," she said. Turning to look at the man in bed beside her, she asked, "You want to shower first or second?"

"How about simultaneously?" he suggested.

She had a feeling that this way would take longer than having them shower separately, but today—and possibly tomorrow—was about them. That meant doing things at their own pace.

Who knew if that could even happen again?

She grinned, running her hand along his face. "Works for me," she announced as she tossed off the sheet that had been tucked around her body.

As she had surmised, it took longer to get ready showering together, but it was also a great deal more rewarding and fun.

It was still early by the time they wound up hitting the road, but they did it fully prepared and looking forward to whatever lay ahead of them.

Danny decided to bring her to Rockefeller Center and then follow that experience up with going on an abbreviated tour of the Museum of Natural History. Because of its size as well as its composition, there was just too much to take in at the museum, but they held hands under the giant shark hanging from the ceiling, strolled casually past dinosaur bones and kissed in the hall of gems and minerals. Cassandra had a feeling that they had barely scratched the surface before Danny had even told her as much.

She could probably spend a month wandering around here, she surmised. Except that she didn't have a month, Cassandra reminded herself.

They ended their little trip with a walk in Central Park, where families were doing their best to play winter games in the fields. Despite the cold, the sky was bright blue and made for a cheery picture.

"This is breathtaking," Cassandra said to the detective.

"I agree."

She realized that Danny was looking directly at her, not at the park. She laughed and shook her head. "You can't possibly compare me to what there is right in front of you," she told him, waving her hand around.

The detective never tore his eyes away from her. "That depends on your definition of *beautiful*."

"This is," she told him, once again waving her hand at the area that surrounded them.

Danny merely smiled at her. "You have your definition of *beautiful* and I have mine," he told her.

Putting his arm around her shoulders, he drew her closer to him. "Are you in the mood to take in any more landmarks?" he asked her. "Or have you had your fill for the day?"

She would have wanted to go on touring the city endlessly, but she really couldn't manage that. "I think you've officially exhausted me," Cassandra told the detective.

"Oh, I certainly hope not," Danny said with genuine feeling. Pressing a kiss to her temple, he told Cassandra, "I know this great little crepe place we could go for dinner. You'll really like it."

"I'm all yours," she told him.

His eyes were saying things to her that made her pulse beat fast. "I certainly hope so," he told her.

She really wished that she could believe him.

What he said sounded absolutely wonderful, but she was convinced that it was one of those spur-of-the-moment responses that rose to a person's lips and was only true for the time being. In the long run, the actual truth of the matter faded, leaving only broken fragments of possibilities in its wake.

"Ready to go home?" Danny asked her after they had finished eating dinner an hour later.

Home.

Danny had said "home." Cassandra knew that she should point out to him that it was his home, not hers.

She should.

But just for tonight, she accepted the use of the term and allowed it to warm her clear down to her toes. How she relished the idea of seeing this wonderful guy every day, every night. They never needed to search for topics to discuss, and the more she learned about him, the stronger her feelings became. It would sting to leave him when this case ended.

No, not sting. *Hurt.*

There was time enough to come to terms with the actual truth of the situation tomorrow. Tonight was for wistful dreams. For forgetting about how they lived on opposite coasts.

"Ready," she answered Danny.

Danny slowly drew back her chair for her, helping her rise to her feet. He had to admit, if just to himself, that he was already anticipating the night that lay ahead.

Chapter 20

She was so beautiful. Even though he wasn't looking directly at her, Danny could feel her presence near him. Her concentration was intense and so was his, usually. Today Danny was having a hard time coping with his wild, out-of-control attraction to her and the idea that she would leave. They had been together for an incredibly short time, Danny thought as he looked up from his work at Cassandra. If he was being honest with himself, the time they had spent together could be thought of as existing in the blink of an eye.

And yet, life had laid itself out for him as existing BC and AC. Life before Cassandra had entered his life and life after she had entered it.

Looking back now, he understood that he had just

been going through the motions, that in reality, he hadn't really been living at all. And now, even sharing a sandwich with her took on a whole new meaning.

The detective caught himself smiling. Suddenly, the very simplest of things meant so much more now than they had before. It occurred to him that prior to Cassandra entering his life, Danny hadn't really been living at all. At least not in the true sense of the word. Without realizing it, he had secretly been waiting for life to catch up with him.

To actually *mean* something.

Yes, Danny quietly acknowledged, he was dedicated to catching the bad guys, to ridding the world of these people who had no regard for life in any sense of the word. But somehow, that wasn't enough. Bringing them to justice didn't make him feel like smiling, like he had done a good job. It was just something that was an offshoot of his having worked a case and doing a decent job.

It wasn't until he had opened himself up to what Cassandra added to his world that he discovered himself finally coming to life. Until that point, he had just been coasting.

Cassandra put down the file she had been going through and working up. For the last hour, she had been compiling more witnesses for them to question and talk to. They had many blocks to walk before this case ended. Keeping herself focused on this killer had to be her number one priority.

But at the moment, the pensive expression on Danny's face had completely captured her attention.

"A penny for your thoughts," Cassandra told him. "Or, judging from the look on your face, my guess is that a dollar fifty would probably be more appropriate."

Caught off guard, Danny blinked. "What?" he asked, clearly confused.

"You look very pensive," Cassandra explained, the file temporarily forgotten. "I was just wondering what you were thinking about."

The corners of Danny's mouth curved. He had been smiling a lot more lately, and that was all thanks to her.

"I'll tell you later—over dinner. Or afterwards," he added sensually.

She could feel herself responding to what he was saying. This man knew how to stir her more than any other man she had ever encountered. Just the way he looked at her excited her. It had been a while since she'd felt any kind of connection to someone. And this guy pushed all her buttons in the best possible way.

Who would have thought that tracking a serial killer could have had this sort of a reward attached to it?

"I plan on holding you to that," she told Danny.

His eyes slid over her, undressing her in his mind. It took him a moment to focus on what she was telling him.

"Deal," he promised. He drew over the file she had been working on and glanced at the names that she had listed. It looked rather complete—for now. "Ready to go out and question more people?" he asked, nodding at the newest list of friends and relatives his team had managed to put together.

Cassandra was already on her feet, reaching for her jacket. "It's what I live for," she told him with a touch of mischief in her voice.

Danny led the way out.

As Cassandra hurried after the detective, the mail clerk, Curtis Wayfare managed to angle his cart so that her path out of the squad room was cut off.

"Sorry," Wayfare apologized flatly, looking anything but repentant. "My bad."

His cutting into her exit had been deliberate, Cassandra thought, frustrated. She couldn't help thinking that she was right. The Wayfare and Wilson were one and the same person She needed to find a way to pin him down and be sure.

"No harm done," she told him after a beat.

They had just entered the hallway. Wayfare was blocking her way to the elevator with his cart.

Okay, enough was enough. "You need to move back," Cassandra told the mail clerk when he just remained standing where he was.

The look in his eyes darkened. "And you need to remember your place," he told her, his voice low, menacing.

Cassandra tossed her head. He was brazen, she'd

give him that. "And where would that be?" she challenged.

"Back to where you came from," he told her nastily. His pasty skin wrinkled in a grimace. "We don't need you parading around here, acting so high and mighty and getting in everyone's way," Wayfare informed her. "The department was doing just fine before you ever came on the scene to stick your nose in all this."

"And just between the two of us," she said, knowing she was pushing his buttons, "I don't think that Detective Doyle shares your opinion about the matter," Cassandra told the mail clerk, aware that the remark would set him off.

Infuriated, Wayfare's complexion turned a deep shade of red. "Of course he does," he all but shouted. And then, regaining his temper, Wayfare lowered his voice as he added, "He's just too polite to say so."

Danny chose that moment to come back, looking for Cassandra.

"What happened to you?" he asked, striding back toward the hallway entrance. "Did you get lost? I thought you were right behind me."

Cassandra saw the nervous, wary look that had come over the mail clerk's features. "I was," she told the detective. Slanting a glance toward Wayfare, she explained, "But then I realized I had forgotten to take something with me, so I had to double back for it."

The expression on the detective's face said he wasn't buying her story. She was up to something, but they were losing time, so he felt he could pick this point up later, when there was more time to explore the various points that needed to be touched upon.

Nodding at the mail clerk by way of taking his leave, Danny took Cassandra's arm and hurried her along.

It wasn't until the detective had her alone in the elevator that Danny finally asked Cassandra, "What was that all about? And don't tell me, 'Nothing,'" he warned. "The look on Wayfare's face said that this was definitely about *something*."

Cassandra debated brushing the detective's question aside, then decided that Danny was not about to let the matter drop easily. Until she was sure, she wasn't going to tell him about her suspicions about the mail clerk.

"He was just being protective."

That didn't make any sense to him. "Of what?" Danny asked.

The elevator opened up and they walked out across the ground floor. "More like of who," she corrected.

"All right," he said gamely, deciding to go that route. "Of who?"

Okay, she thought with an inward sigh. The man had asked for it. Her eyes met his. "You."

Eyebrows drew together so closely, they all but made a single arched, dark brown line.

"Me?" he questioned, clearly stunned. "Why was Wayfare being protective of me?" It just didn't make any sense to the detective. She had to be mistaken.

She bit her tongue. "To save you from me, I would imagine," Cassandra answered.

Danny shook his head as he began walking again, heading toward the parking garage. "You've lost me, Cass. What are you talking about?"

He didn't see it, she thought. But then, that would take his admitting that he was the object of the mail clerk's affection, and Danny clearly didn't think in those terms. That sort of blatant adoration was hard enough for the detective to accept, much less admit to himself that he had somehow managed to miss all the signs.

Cassandra gave the detective a good onceover. She could easily see why the mail clerk had been drawn to Danny. Not only was the man easy to be around, but he was also kind to everyone. His team-mates respected him and sought him out through-out the day, not just to discuss details of the case but just to talk. And while Danny may have been an astute detective, he downgraded his own influence on others.

Still, she felt she had to at least make Danny aware of the situation with Curtis Wayfare. "For lack of a better word right now, I'd say that that Wayfare and Wilson are one and the same person. And he apparently has some kind of attachment to you." She slanted a look in his direction. "I vote that we begin gathering more information on him. It could be entirely benign, but I think we really need to check him out."

It made the detective uncomfortable to admit it, but she just might have a point, Danny decided. Still right now they couldn't just drop everything else to exclusively focus on only Wayfare/Wilson, because they could be wrong and the real serial killer could go scot-free.

Danny did make a mental note to look into the matter further. He couldn't afford to just shrug the matter off. Cassandra wouldn't push the matter to this degree if she didn't believe that there was something there.

For now, he thought, he and the team would continue to focus on the new list that had been compiled. There was no shortage of people to visit and interview.

Distributing the list, the detective made sure that each member of his team had the same number of people to talk to and investigate.

"You know, I'm really beginning to feel like a dog that's trying to chase its own tail," Cassandra said as she got back into Danny's car. They had just finished talking to someone professing to be a close friend of one of the newest victims that had been discovered.

He looked at her for a second. "Now that's rather an interesting image to consider," Danny commented, pulling out of the parking that was located across the street from the person they had been questioning.

As always, there was traffic. He made his way

slowly down the block and back onto a bustling avenue. "Care to explain why?"

"Because no matter how much energy is used, all we seem to be able to do is go around in circles—which wind up taking us absolutely nowhere."

"Not all of the cases we work are going to be neatly wrapped up in a bow," he told her, then sighed, struggling to keep the disappointment out of his voice. "A lot of these cases are *never* solved."

She nodded. He was not telling her anything new. "I know, but I still can't seem to shake this feeling that we're overlooking something. That we're staring at the answer right in the face and just not seeing it."

He shrugged, allowing his vehicle to idle as he waited for the light to change. "Maybe you're right." And then he added, "Hang on to that feeling."

"Oh, I fully intend to," Cassandra told him. She hadn't flown three thousand miles from one coast to the other just to fail.

"Okay," he said, resigned to continue going down the list. "Who's next?"

She had held on to the list and glanced down now. "Albert Walker. He's a retired engineer who lives in Queens." She ratted off the address that was written right next to the man's name.

Danny nodded, familiar with the area. At least, he had been when he was younger.

But when they finally arrived at a crumbling single-family home that looked as if it had been constructed just at the end of the Civil War, it was

nothing like he had remembered. The painfully
thin woman who came to the door in response to
his knock told them that Albert Walker had recently
sold the house and had moved to Florida.

"Did he give you a number where he could be
reached?" Danny asked her.

The woman, Gloria, shook her head. "I think he
was afraid that I would call him to say I changed
my mind and ask for my money back." She smiled,
showing off her brand-new dental work. It was clear
that she was very pleased with herself. "He didn't
know about the developer who was buying up the
entire block. His loss, my gain," Gloria declared tri-
umphantly.

"And you're sure you don't know how to get in
touch with Albert Walker?" Cassandra asked. This
could be the one person who mattered, she couldn't
help thinking.

"Perfectly."

With that, Gloria closed the door before they could
ask any more questions.

Danny blew out a frustrated breath as they made
their way back to his vehicle. "Okay, next person,"
the detective said wearily. He noticed that Cassandra
seemed to fall back before they reached the automo-
bile. "Something wrong?" he asked, looking around
the general vicinity.

Cassandra pressed her lips together, wondering
if she should say anything to him. He would probably think she was just imagining things or being

paranoid. Maybe she was, but for the past day, she couldn't seem to shake the feeling that they were being watched—and most likely followed. At first, she was certain it was all in her head, but the gut-wrenching feeling continued, growing more intense as the day grew longer.

"I don't know. Maybe it's nothing," she responded.

"But?" Danny prodded, waiting for her to tell him what was really bothering her. "C'mon, Cavanaugh," he said, unlocking the doors to the car. However, for now he remained standing next to the vehicle. "Out with it."

"You're going to think I'm being crazy. Again," she added since she had already admitted to having this feeling before.

"I'll let you know if I do—or not," he told her.

Cassandra blew out a breath. "All right, you asked for this." She drew in a breath, then said, "I think we're being followed. It's a gut feeling more than anything else," she admitted. "But every time I turn around, I could swear I just missed seeing the person who's following us."

To her relief, Danny didn't laugh at her. He listened to her elaborate a little on her admission, then said, "The next time you feel like someone's watching us, give me a signal." Then, before she could ask what sort of signal, he told her, "Take my hand."

"All right," she agreed. "But this just might be you, getting a little spicy on me."

"Hey, I have to find a way to break up the monotony somehow," he deadpanned.

For a second, she felt as if the tension had dissipated to a degree.

But only for a second.

The next moment, that tense, uneasy feeling that haunted her returned to continue to shadow her.

When he brought his vehicle to a stop at a red light, Danny glanced in her direction. He noticed the way Cassandra was covering the sidearm at her hip with her hand. He sensed that she wanted to be ready, just in case.

"You can feel him, can't you?" he asked.

"It's probably just my imagination," she told him with a shrug.

"I know it's only been a short while, but I've learned to trust your imagination," Danny told her. "You'll have two sets of eyes on the alert and watching instead of just one set," he told her.

She was not sure if he was just humoring her or not, but the detective knew how to make her feel better, Cassandra thought, taking comfort in his assurance.

They went on to another name on the list, making a real effort to find and question the person.

Edward Heller turned out to be exceedingly cooperative. A librarian by trade, he gave the impression that he was very aware of his surroundings.

But in the end, after questioning the man, they

were no closer to solving the puzzle they were at-tempting to reconstruct than they had initially been.

And the feeling, of someone following them, re-fused to abate.

Cassandra comforted herself with the thought that this could mean that they were getting closer to fi-nally finding the serial killer. It was just a matter of time, she promised herself—and hoped that she wasn't wrong.

Chapter 21

"Don't take this the wrong way, but the streets of your city really make me nervous after dark," Cassandra told the detective walking at her side.

"You're just not used to them. Don't believe the hype."

"Yeah, but dark city streets are still great places to commit crimes."

"We are trained to deal with them, remember?" Danny said with a teasing light in his eyes.

"Thanks for reminding me." She hoped she conveyed sarcasm, but maybe he really believed that she might be afraid. Not afraid, just on her guard. It wasn't the worst quality to have in a detective and had saved her butt on numerous occasions.

Danny leaned in closer as they made their way

up the street. The temperature had dropped again, the wind had picked up, and it was practically close to freezing.

They had one more person to talk to on their list for the day. Could this be the one who would break open the case for them? That was always the question and why they kept going for hours on end.

Danny had come close to calling it a night right after they had finished interviewing the previous person, Raul Chan, but Cassandra wanted to talk to this last witness.

"This way, we can start fresh in the morning," she told him.

The detective had a different view of the situation. "Maybe we'll get lucky, and Jason Bradford won't be home," Danny said as he led the way to the unlit apartment building.

Cassandra kept looking around, memorizing her surroundings. She was trying to remain alert to any sort of possibilities that might wind up transpiring.

As she and Danny drew closer to the building, she could feel her pulse quickening in anticipation. No matter what Danny said, she could sense something was up. It could very well be her imagination. Cops often had a sixth sense about upcoming scenes and this was one of those times. She knew they wouldn't go home so quickly after this next visit.

"Funny how the lack of light can make some places appear absolutely creepy," Cassandra couldn't help commenting.

Danny totally agreed with her insight. "No argument there. City funding when it comes to better lighting in all neighborhoods has been slow going. In the meantime, I like the summers here. It might be hot and sticky, and at times a total mosquito-fest, but at least the light does last longer. Cuts down a bit on the creepiness," he added. "So, I guess in a way, it's a tradeoff."

"Are you trying to distract me, Detective?"

"Hey, if it helps…"

The detective glanced down at his cell phone. The last address on their list had been sent to him by an assistant a few minutes ago.

He frowned as he read the address and then looked up at the building they were standing in front of. It resembled a neglected Gothic hotel, with shadows, faint lights in windows and the promise of cobwebs and creepy corners inside.

"This is it." Danny glanced at the woman accompanying him. "This doesn't look very hospitable, does it?" he asked, commenting on the way the building looked. "Would you rather come back tomorrow morning instead of going in tonight?"

Just as they had approached the building, Danny had noticed that the lights corresponding to Jason Bradford's apartment were not on. For the second time, the detective thought that it might be a better idea to approach Jason Bradford's apartment when they were all fresh.

But Cassandra didn't share his view of the matter. "We're here. We might as well see if the man is in."

Danny sighed, nodding. "I had a feeling you were going to say that."

Amused, Cassandra glanced at him. "Am I really all that predictable?"

"Just to me," Danny told her with a broad wink. With that, he proceeded into the building and up the elevator to the right floor. The decor didn't get any less creepy with its peeling paint and patchy carpeting on the floors. Danny leaned forward to ring the outdoor apartment's doorbell. When there was no corresponding sound, he decided that the doorbell was more than likely broken, so he knocked instead.

Twice.

No one answered.

Danny decided that there was no one home, or at least no one who was willing to answer at this hour. Either way, he felt that there was only one course open to him.

"Looks like we're coming back in the morning after all," Danny said.

But just as he was about to turn on his heel to walk away, Cassandra caught him by the arm, holding him in place. When he looked at her quizzically, she nodded toward the apartment. "Did you hear that?"

"Hear what?" Danny asked.

"I could swear there was a sound coming from the inside the apartment," she answered, then urged, "Listen."

Danny was inclined to dismiss her words as being the product of her imagination when he took a closer look at Cassandra. More to the point, he saw the expression on her face.

"You're actually being serious," the detective realized.

"Of course I'm serious," Cassandra insisted, lowering her voice. She nodded toward the door, then repeated, "Listen."

So he did, cocking his head and concentrating. This time, Danny thought he picked up a very faint noise coming from inside the apartment.

"Maybe a window was left open," he theorized.

"And maybe someone isn't answering for a reason," she countered. Specifically, she thought maybe whoever was in the apartment didn't want to talk to anyone.

"There could be a lot of reasons for that," Danny told her.

She saw no reason to argue the point. "True," Cassandra agreed, then completely threw him when she said, "Could be a thief, ransacking the place. I'd say it's up to us to check it out."

Danny was beginning to know her looks. "You're not going to give up until I agree," he surmised. "We'll have to bring in the landlord so they can use their keys."

"No need," she informed him as she took out a long, thin sliver of metal and proceeded to utilize it. The next thing Danny knew, she had managed to unlock the front door of Jason Bradford's apartment.

As he had already determined, there were no lights on, but from the sound they had detected, there was definitely someone there.

Danny took the lead, motioning to Cassandra to follow him as he slowly made his way toward the next room and the source of the noise.

Everything happened lightning fast from that point on.

There was a tall, thin man in the shadows. He was bending over Jason Bradford, the prone figure on the floor and was obviously startled as he jumped.

Cursing, he shifted his attention from what he was doing to the two people who had caught him at it. Even in the dim light, the hatred in his eyes was definitely noticeable.

"Damn it!" the man cried, following the exclamation with a number of other, far more ripe expressions of vile anger. It was then that Danny noticed the man was holding a knife in his hand. The sharp weapon was bloodstained.

The next second, he lunged at Danny, determined to sink the knife into his flesh.

Horrified, Cassandra recognized the mail clerk just as she attempted to stop him by pushing him out of the way. The killer tossed her aside as if she were a mere rag doll. Landing, on the floor, she wound up hitting her head against a cabinet.

Dizzy, she tried to clear her head while she was still on the floor. Every bone in her body ached as she reached for her weapon. Cassandra was very aware of the fact that she had only a few seconds to stop this man from committing yet another murder.

Or two.

Infuriated, Curtis Wayfare had raised his knife high in the air, determined to do the maximum amount of damage when he wound up making contact with Danny's body.

Only he didn't make contact.

At the last possible moment, Cassandra screamed out a warning, then as the serial killer spun around, about to plunge the knife into her, she fired.

Discharging her weapon rapidly, she managed to hit Wayfare/Wilson in the chest, in his left shoulder and in his head.

The killer fell with a thud at her feet. His last conscious act was to attempt to grab her in order to remain upright.

There was a scream, and it took Cassandra a moment to realize that the sound had torn from her own lips, encapsulating the horror she had just experienced.

Danny seized his weapon, pointing it at Wayfare/Wilson, ready to shoot. But there was no need to discharge it again.

The serial killer was dead, as was his latest victim.

Danny's eyes swept over Cassandra, more concerned than he had ever been in his life.

"Are you all right?" They asked the question simultaneously, then laughed as their voices, still mingling, replied, "Yes."

Lodged protectively in the detective's arms, Cassandra cast an uneasy look at the man on the floor, blood pooling and swiftly leaving his body.

"Are we sure he's dead?" she asked, staring at the killer and watching for him to make a move—*any* move.

"Unless he belongs to one of the undead, I'd say, yes, he's most assuredly dead."

Reluctantly releasing Cassandra for a moment, Danny took out his phone and quickly called for an ambulance, giving his badge and ID number to dispatch, along with a quick summation of what had happened.

Ending the call, he put his cell phone into his pocket. "The ambulance should be here soon," he told her.

Cassandra looked down at the deceased serial killer and his victim. "I don't think that'll make much of a difference to either one of them."

"The ambulance is for you," Danny told her, then watched as Cassandra's shoulders stiffened.

"I don't need an ambulance," she said to the detective despite the fact that her head insisted on spinning.

Taking out his handkerchief, Danny wiped away the blood on her forehead. She had managed to hit it in two places. Holding the handkerchief up for Cassandra to see, he said, "I beg to differ with you, Detective Cavanaugh. You most definitely need to be checked out. I'm not letting anything happen to you on my watch," he told her. "Now stop arguing with me and just rest until the ambulance gets here." He could hear the siren in the distance. "Which, from the sound of it, will be any minute now."

Woozy, Cassandra blew out a breath. She hated having a fuss made over her. "This is a waste of time." Although, to be honest, her legs started to feel weak, not to mention that her head was still spinning.

"And it's my time to waste," he informed her. "I thought you California girls were supposed to be easygoing."

"We are," she responded in a crisp voice.

"Arguing is not easygoing," Danny said.

Just then, they heard the ambulance pulling up. The next moment, there was a knock on the door, and two paramedics came in, pushing a stretcher between them.

Danny felt it only fair to warn the ambulance attendants, "She's going to tell you that she doesn't need to go to the hospital. Don't listen to her."

And then he pointed toward the dead serial killer and his victim lying on the ground. "No hurry with them, they're both dead. But FYI, that one," he indicated thedead mail clerk, "is the serial killer everyone's been living in fear of ever since those bodies were found buried within the construction site."

The shorter of the two paramedics crossed over toward the dead serial killer. "Doesn't look all that the scary now, does he?"

"He was scary enough to kill all those people over the years and get away with it," Cassandra said, her voice fading a little. "He had been slaying men for much too long. Someone should have caught on before now," she told them. "But the trouble was that this guy looked almost harmless and much too fussy to represent the kind of danger that he was actually capable of."

That was when the paramedic waved over his partner, who brought the stretcher over toward Cassandra. "Time to take you to the hospital to check you out, Detective." He indicated that she needed to get onto the stretcher.

Cassandra tried one last time. "I'm fine," she protested.

"The rest of us want to make sure that's the actual case. You're not going to deny that to us now, are you?" he asked Cassandra.

She was of a mind to go on protesting that she was fine, except that she suddenly became really dizzy.

The sensation only grew stronger, and rather quickly at that. She caught herself clutching at Danny as her knees began to buckle, threatening to make her collapse.

That was when a pair of strong arms caught her, then gently put her onto the stretcher. Things began to grow increasingly distant as well as blurry.

And then suddenly, everything shrank down to the size of a pinprick, after which it completely disappeared.

When Cassandra came to, she found herself lying in a hospital bed. Not only that, but she was wearing a hospital gown. Sunlight streamed through the window blinds.

Danny was sitting beside her. When he saw her opening her eyes, he was instantly on his feet, relieved to see color coming back to her face. "Welcome back," he told her.

"Where are my clothes?" she asked, uncomfortable to find herself like this.

"We held a raffle," he told her.

She blinked, attempting to focus. "What?"

"Don't worry," he told her, taking her hand. "Your clothes are in the closet." He indicated the closet next to the bathroom in the front of the hospital room. "But they're going to be taking you to get some X-rays and an MRI shortly, so you won't be needing your clothes for a while."

Danny could see the protest forming on her lips. He fell back on the logical excuse. "They have to check you out, Cass. They don't want to risk being sued because they merrily sent you on your way," he told her. "And as for me, I want to be able to continue making love with you without worrying that you're suddenly going to expire on me in the middle of it all."

She put her hand to her forehead, as if that would help her make sense out of what she had just heard. "Continue making love?" she repeated, mystified.

"Well, yeah—unless you've already grown tired of me," he said, hoping that hadn't become the case.

"No, I haven't grown tired of you," she said, not really believing she was having this conversation with him. It all felt rather unreal to her. How was it that she wound up here with Danny at her side?

"Good, because the minute they give you a clean bill of health, you can show me just how not tired of me you are," he told her with a warm grin.

"Okay," she said just as a nurse came in to take her down for her workup.

Cassandra found herself clutching to the arms of the wheelchair as she prepared to be pushed out of the room. This was not the time to point out that with this serial killer put out of the city's misery, she and Travis would be on their way back to Aurora, most likely very soon.

But that was still in the future, no matter how close that future might be. Moreover, for now, she needed to focus on not having the world dance around in her head. Even the light in the room seemed a little too bright.

"Will you be here when they bring me back?" she asked the detective as the nurse started wheeling her out of the room.

He laughed at the question. "Like you could dynamite me out of here."

Cassandra nodded. "Good. Definitely not planning on doing that," she told him. She didn't like not being in good enough shape to walk on her own. But even she could admit that she needed some help and a whole lot of TLC.

Chapter 22

It continued to be the story of the hour. Coupled with the human interest angle that finding their cousin's killer—Nathan could finally be sent home to rest—was ending the threat of a serial killer roaming the streets of the most exciting city in the country, possibly the world, brought with it a huge collective sigh of relief.

Cassandra could almost swear that she was able to hear it as she lay in the detective's arms a week later. There was a constant lull of city noise and cheering around the police precinct that had cracked the case. Every now and then, members of the team, with chests puffed out, would go outside to give interviews about the work involved in tracking this killer.

As for Cassandra, she had been released from the

hospital with a clean bill of health, then had spent the rest of the time dodging eager reporters who were looking to write the next Pulitzer Prize winning story based on the capture and elimination of the serial killer who had been haunting the city for such a long time. A few reporters asked for details of Nathan's life, something she felt was too private to talk about even if she were so inclined. There was even talk of a limited series starring several promising actors.

"You know, you're missing a great opportunity to be immortalized as the detective who rode in from California on a surfboard to save a bunch of New Yorkers from suffering at the hands of a deadly, cold-blooded killer."

Cassandra curled up against the detective. "It's not as if I didn't have help. A *lot* of help," she emphasized, looking up at him from her vantage point.

But he shook his head. "I just got into this after you saw what was going on. You were the one who honed in on Wayfare with that gut feeling of yours."

"What can I say?" she asked, smiling at Danny. "You bring out the best in me."

This was a truth she'd come to accept. Working with Danny had helped her delve more deeply into a case, scout out every possible clue no matter how obscure. It made her feel…creative. In a family of law enforcement, one could easily fall into a way of operating that was the opposite of creative. But Cassandra knew her gift was imagining scenarios that might not be likely but could be. This was how she knew to follow her gut on this case…and work with Danny.

"Ditto. You've helped me be a better detective, that's for sure," he told her with a smile. And then the smile faded a little as he thought about the near future. "You're going to be leaving soon, aren't you?" The words tasted extremely bitter on his tongue. "Going back to Aurora, right?"

Without realizing it, her arm tightened around his chest as she attempted to deal with the situation. "That was the plan, yes," Cassandra responded. Now that this was all over and the killer had been caught, she and Travis were supposed to be scheduled to go back home. Nathan's remains has already been shipped, preceding them.

So, why did going back to the West Coast, back to everyone she had ever loved and cared about, feel so wrong to her right now? Every time she tried to envision leaving her family, she forced herself to ditch the idea. But leaving Danny seemed just as ludicrous and, yes, wrong.

Cassandra let out a long, shaky sigh, which encouraged the detective to continue talking, continue voicing the idea that had been forming in his head for a while now. It hadn't jelled until just recently, spurred on by seeing Cassandra lying in that hospital bed and realizing that he could have very well lost her permanently. And what that would have felt like if he had.

He saw himself wandering city streets like a zombie and going back to coasting through life. He could make a life solving case after case and obeying the needs of his work. But something had changed in such a short time. Was that even possible?

The idea of going through the motions for the next forty years was suddenly unacceptable. No way could he do this without Cassandra by his side, her upbeat attitude nudging him into the day.

"Would you happen to know if there's any place in that precinct where you work for another cop, or more to the point, perhaps another police detective?" he asked.

Cassandra felt her heart suddenly flutter as she drew herself up to look at the man beside her. Was he saying what she thought he was saying, or was he just extrapolating on information he had just happened to hear? Maybe her injuries had taken a toll on her.

She would hate to ask and put herself out there only to be disappointed. The smart thing would be just to coast and let him keep on talking, eventually getting enough information to draw a conclusion.

But she didn't feel like being smart or cautious. Coming face-to-face with an actual serial killer and surviving that encounter had a way of negating all her previous underpinnings of caution. There was only this life, and she wanted it to be with him.

"Are you asking for yourself?" she asked.

"And if I was?" he posed.

He *was* asking for himself, she thought, everything within her rejoicing.

"I'd find a way to get someone to retire in order to get a good position for you," she told him. Cassandra sat up, looking at him. "I am sure that you would be a welcome addition to the Aurora police force. Uncle Brian is always looking for a good man to join up." Excitement had caused her mind to scramble and fog up. It took her a second to be able to get her thoughts in order. "As a matter of fact, I know of at least two positions that are due to open up when Hotchkiss and Evans retire."

"Hotchkiss and Evans?" Danny repeated slowly.

"Two long-time detectives who have put in their papers and are set to retire," she told him. And then she realized that she was getting ahead of herself. "You *are* thinking of something permanent, right? Or is this just a passing fancy that you're thinking of exploring in the short run?"

His eyes were already making love to her. "That all depends."

She ordered her heart to settle down. It didn't listen. "On?"

He lightly kissed her temple. "On whether or not I can get a certain very sexy homicide detective to tell me how she feels about the idea of having me transfer to her precinct. I don't want to intrude if you just want to keep all the Cavanaughs to yourself. I mean, I get it if this is too sudden and you—"

"Sexy?" she repeated, surprised. "You think I'm sexy?"

"Oh, hell yes," Danny answered. "I might have missed all those initial signs pointing to Wayfare being the serial killer we were hunting, but that doesn't mean I'm totally blind."

She laughed, throwing her arms around Danny's neck. "You really have the strangest way of complimenting a person, but I will definitely take it," she told him happily just before she sealed her lips to his.

It took her a while before she was able to draw her lips back again, as well as catch her breath so that she was able to put a question to him.

"So, I take it you'll be transferring to the Aurora Police Department?" she asked him hopefully.

"As soon as I can put in my papers," he said.

It all sounded wonderful, but she had been taught a long time ago not to count her chickens before the eggs were at least laid, much less hatched.

"What if you don't like it there?" she questioned, then felt herself start to babble excitedly. "I mean, Aurora is like a paradise with mountains in the north, both urban and rural delights, good restaurants, lots of Cavanaughs, of course. But I'm sure New York is way too exciting to leave even though you have these really cold winters and probably not a lot of tanning opportunities."

"You're going to be there, right?" he said to Cassandra.

It seemed like an odd question to ask her, but she answered anyway. "That's a given."

"Then I'll love it," he assured her.

"But—"

"Cavanaugh," he said, drawing her back into his arms and nibbling on her ear.

She breathed, her pulse racing madly. Dreams did come true. Who would have thought? That's why it paid to be an optimist. "Yes?"

"Stop talking. I've got much better things for your lips to be doing," he told her and then proceeded to show her exactly what he meant.

Her heart pounding hard, she found herself agreeing with him totally.

* * * * *

Don't forget previous titles in the
Cavanaugh Justice series:

Cavanaugh Justice: Up Close and Deadly
Cavanaugh Justice: Deadly Chase
Cavanaugh Justice: Serial Affair
Cavanaugh Justice: The Baby Trail
Cavanaugh in Plain Sight
Cavanaugh Stakeout

Available now from
Harlequin Romantic Suspense!

#2223 COLTON'S BODY OF PROOF
The Coltons of New York • by Karen Whiddon
Officer Ellie Mathers just spotted her high school best friend...
who's been missing for sixteen years. Reuniting with ex
Liam Colton is the only way to solve the mystery. But is Ellie's
biggest threat the flying bullets targeting her...or the sparks
still flying between her and Liam?

#2224 OPERATION WITNESS PROTECTION
Cutter's Code • by Justine Davis
Twisted family secrets are exposed when Case McMillan
saves a woman from an attack. But Terri Johnson's
connection to the powerful Foxworth Foundation is only the
beginning. She's now in a murderer's crosshairs, challenging
everything, from Case's former job as a cop to his carefully
guarded heart.

#2225 COLD CASE SHERIFF
Sierra's Web • by Tara Taylor Quinn
Aimee Barker has had nightmares since her parents' murder.
Now she's being shot at! Sheriff Jackson Redmond vows to
protect the vulnerable beauty and help her solve the cold
case. But can he offer the loving home she craves once his
connection to the suspect is revealed?

#2226 HER K-9 PROTECTOR
Big Sky Justice • by Kimberly Van Meter
Single mom Kenna Griffin is running from a dangerous ex. But
her fresh start is complicated by K-9 cop Lucas Merritt...and
her deepening feelings for him. She's scared to trust him with
her love and her dark secrets. Keeping them hidden could
get them both killed...

HARLEQUIN PLUS

Try the best multimedia subscription service for romance readers like you!

Read, Watch and Play.

Experience the easiest way to get the romance content you crave.

Start your **FREE TRIAL** at
<u>www.harlequinplus.com/freetrial</u>.